CRITICAL PRAISE FOR LYN COTE

On FINALLY FOUND
"Lyn Cote blends strong writing with
an interesting cast to create an entertaining,
memorable story."
—*Romantic Times*

On NEVER ALONE
"A lively story big on plot, powerful
emotion and strong characterization, this
irresistible tales showcases the talent
of a thrilling new author."
—*Romantic Times*

On FINALLY HOME
"This is possibly Ms. Cote's best yet
for Love Inspired."
—*Romantic Times*

On HIS SAVING GRACE
"Lyn Cote expertly pens a compelling novel
of work, family and love."
—*Romantic Times*

* * *

Lyn Cote's SISTERS OF THE HEART series:

Gracie's story—
His Saving Grace (LI #247, 4/04)

Patience's story—
Testing His Patience (LI #255, 6/04)

Connie's story—
Loving Constance (LI #277, 11/04)

Books by Lyn Cote

Love Inspired

Never Alone #30
New Man in Town #66
Hope's Garden #111
Finally Home #137
Finally Found #162
The Preacher's Daughter #221
His Saving Grace #247
Testing His Patience #255
Loving Constance #277

*Sisters of the Heart

LYN COTE

now lives in Wisconsin with her husband, her real-life hero. They raised a son and daughter together. Lyn has spent her adult life as a schoolteacher, a full-time mom and now a writer. Lyn's favorite food is watermelon. Realizing that this delicacy is only available one season out of the year, Lyn's friends keep up a constant flow of "watermelon" gifts—candles, wood carvings, pillows, cloth bags, candy and on and on. Lyn also enjoys crocheting and knitting, watching *Wheel of Fortune* and doing lunch with friends. By the way, Lyn's last name is pronounced "Coty."

Lyn enjoys hearing from readers, who can contact her at P.O. Box 864, Woodruff, WI 54568 or by e-mail at l.cote@juno.com.

LOVING CONSTANCE

LYN COTE

Steeple
Hill®

Published by Steeple Hill Books™

STEEPLE HILL BOOKS

Steeple
Hill®

ISBN 0-373-87287-9

LOVING CONSTANCE

www.SteepleHill.com

Printed in U.S.A.

When I was a child, my speech, feelings and thinking were all those of a child; now that I am a man, I have no more use for childish ways.

—*1 Corinthians* 13:11

To my new critique group in Woodruff,
Wisconsin. Thanks for all your encouragement.
And the same to my friends of HIFA,
Heart of Iowa Fiction Authors!

Chapter One

Friday evening, Connie Oberlin wasn't nervous about the party in her honor until she turned the last corner into her old Chicago neighborhood. Then she realized she had only been lying to herself. The sight of Annie and Troy's house brought back feelings better left untouched.

Late June sunshine glinted on her windshield as she edged her Volvo into a space along the narrow alley. Tonight would be fun. Tonight would be tense, but only to her. His face flickered in her unwilling mind. Yes, she would see him tonight. Caution whispered through her.

Her soul felt a guilty tug. *Lord, I've guarded my heart and mind. I've done nothing that would dishonor You. Please lead me away from temptation as You have in the past.* She closed her eyes and took a deep breath, marshaling her resistance. *You'd think*

I'd be over the last traces of my infatuation by now.
But these words didn't ring true.

She slowly got out and then walked through the
gate into the backyard. And was mobbed.

Her oldest and dearest friends, Annie and her sister Gracie and their cousin Patience, threw their arms
around her and squealed—just as they had as girls.
Dropping her purse and weekend bag, Connie
laughed out loud and leaned into the hearty four-way
hug, though she towered a head taller than the petite,
brunette sisters. Willowy, blond Patience and she
were the tall ones.

Standing by the grill, Annie's father waved and
shouted, "Hey, Connie! Big-time lawyer!" Patience's
brand-new husband, tall and dark and handsome,
stood beside him.

Annie and Troy's five-year-old twin sons leaped
from their backyard swing and pelted toward Connie. They hugged her around her knees and shouted,
"Aunt Connie's here! What'd you bring us?"

Annie pried the blond duo off Connie and scolded
them. "You better be glad your father isn't home on
time. He hates it when you two beg."

Connie ruffled the twins' bowl-cut bangs. Her
heart riotous, she scanned the gaily decorated backyard. Clusters of colorful Mylar balloons, tethered
to the fence and back porch, bounced on the summer
breezes. Picnic tables were decked out in white ta-
blecloths. Bowls of food brought by the neighbors

completely covered one table. She watched as Patience went to stand beside her husband who put a loving arm around her. Gracie's husband stood by his wife, too. She was so happy for Patience and Gracie. Why did all this make her want to cry?

In the warmth of late-afternoon sun, she scooped her shoulder-length brown hair into a ponytail and excused herself. She'd thought ahead and had brought a change of clothes with her. She walked into the white frame two-flat that she'd lived next to as a child and which had been a second home to her all her life. After remarrying recently, Gracie's father had moved away to his wife's home. So Gracie and her husband lived in the downstairs flat now, while Annie and Troy still lived upstairs with the twins.

Inside the downstairs bathroom, Connie changed out of her three-piece suit into cooler and casual cropped jeans and an off-white cotton top. She stared at her somber reflection in the mirror, trying to get into a party mood, to prepare herself to smile at him and show no other reaction than friendship. *Lord, I want that to be true.* Of their own accord, her eyes drifted to the alley again, waiting to see Troy walk through the gate.

She strolled back outside, smiling with difficulty. But old neighbors distracted her from her nervousness, crowding around her, hugging her, kissing her cheek. "Congratulations on passing the bar" was repeated over and over as well as "We knew you could do it." Connie returned the hugs and kisses and forced herself to ask about children and grandchildren.

Finally, Troy's uncle arrived. Uncle Lou, Troy's mother's brother, owned the large construction company Troy worked for. Lou thumped Connie on the back with his meaty paw and beamed his pleasure. Then he turned and boomed across the crowded yard to Annie, "Where's that husband of yours? I told him to leave the job in Taperville early tonight and get home here."

"Yeah, tell him to get here fast," Annie's father agreed. "The burgers are almost done!"

"I'll call his cell phone again." Annie reached into her jean pocket and pulled out her own phone.

As the twins dragged Connie over to the swing set so she could push them high, she watched Annie grimace as she hung up. Obviously she'd gotten no answer. Connie propelled the twins' swings in turn, listening to their shouts of pleasure. And wondered what was keeping Troy.

More neighbors arrived. Annie's dad started scooping burgers off the grill onto waiting buns. The neighbor ladies uncovered bowls and the buffet began. Connie and everyone else watched for Troy. Every few minutes, Annie took out her cell phone, people lowered their voices, murmuring, "What's keeping him? This isn't like Troy." In equal measures, Connie felt relief at not having to face him and concern for his safety and…self-reproach larger than both.

Finally, Connie led the twins over to the food and helped them fill their plates. "Where's Daddy?" one asked her.

"Don't worry, your daddy will be here soon," she murmured.

Minutes, hours passed; neighbors crowded around the tables laughing, talking, toasting Connie on her passing the bar and on Patience and Gil's recent wedding. But worry hung over everyone— where was Troy? With a brittle smile in place, Connie cut the sheet cake and posed for a myriad of photos. Still, he didn't show.

The sun blazed golden-pink to the west as the long summer twilight advanced. Annie's dad lit the citronella torches to ward off mosquitoes. Annie's face became more drawn and her smile more stiff.

Where are you, Troy? Connie saw this question mirrored in the faces around her. As the first tinge of darkness clouded the sky, the party atmosphere became strained. As Annie tried Troy's cell number yet again, Gracie leaned close to Connie. "This isn't like Troy. I'm worried."

Connie nodded, her mood sinking with the dying sun.

Hours later, well past midnight, only Connie, Annie and Gracie huddled around the kitchen table upstairs in Annie and Troy's apartment. Their sons slept down the hall in their bedroom. Connie had called all the hospitals between the job site in Taperville and home. Though she wouldn't be able to file a formal missing person's report, she'd also called the local precinct to report Troy's not coming home and had given his description and his vehicle's license plate. Friends and relatives were out searching for Troy or at home praying for him. Patience had gone out looking with her husband Gil, who was a stranger to Chicago. Why hadn't Troy come home tonight?

"I can't believe this is happening," Annie mumbled. "Stuff like this only happens on TV to other people."

Stiff with fear, Connie met Annie's dark, anxious eyes. "It will be all right," Connie repeated the empty words.

Annie stood, scraping her chair backward. "You keep saying that," she said, her voice crackling with tension. "But there isn't any way that something hasn't happened to Troy. We didn't have a fight. He knew about the party tonight and was looking forward to it. He couldn't have just *forgotten* he had a family and a celebration waiting for him. He'd have called hours ago if he'd had car trouble. Something's *happened.*" Her voice broke on the last word.

Connie and Gracie rose as one to embrace Annie, who'd covered her face with her hands.

The doorbell downstairs in the joint foyer of the two-flat rang. The three of them froze in place. "Who would be here at this hour?" Gracie asked.

No one but the police would be at their door at this late hour. Connie saw this fact strike Gracie and then Annie. "I'll go and see who it is," Connie said in a rush. "Maybe it's one of the guys. One of them might have forgotten their key." She left Gracie holding Annie close. Because neither of them thought anyone had forgotten a key.

Descending the stairs to the foyer to face—who knew what—gave Connie the sensation of sliding down a cliff. Tears gathered in her throat, which she struggled to swallow. In the foyer, she flicked on the light and saw through the door's window the outline of two men.

She kept the chain lock in place and opened the door a crack. Even though somehow expected, the sight of a blue uniform on one of the two men slammed through her. Her heart in free-fall, she hit bottom, landing winded and weak. "No," she whispered. *Annie can't have lost Troy.*

The uniformed officer showed her a badge. "Is this the residence of Troy Nielsen?" he asked.

She jerked her head in a facsimile of a nod. Her hands trembling, she slid the chain lock open and stepped back to let them in.

The second man, not in uniform—tall, lean and dark-haired—followed the policeman in. She stared at his shadowed face. It appeared all lines and planes, no roundness, no softness in him.

Rand O'Neill had been notifying next of kin for years. On the way here, he'd tightened his self-control to shield himself from the dark and swirling reactions he'd meet here tonight. Why didn't this ever become routine to him? He knew the reason. Gritting his teeth, he slammed shut that door to his own past.

The young woman standing before him suddenly blanched. He reached out and gripped her slender arm. "You look faint." He felt her resistance to his help, the way she held herself rigidly. Then she swayed.

He tightened his grasp. For a few moments, she leaned toward him, letting him brace her. He noticed the way the overhead light glinted, playing up the red sheen in her thick brown hair and the way she fought giving in to shock. He hung on to her, trying to give her strength.

Then she shook and wrested herself from him. "I'm okay." She warned him away with raised palms. "It's just…all the hours…it's late. Have you found Troy?"

This wasn't his cue. Rand remained silent but his hands still tingled where they'd touched her skin.

"Who are you, miss?" Hess, the uniformed officer, cut in.

"Connie Oberlin, a friend of the family." She wrapped her arms around herself.

Rand considered the surroundings and her, listening to her voice, uncertain yet strong. He took inventory of her attractive face and figure.

"Is Mrs. Nielsen here?" Hess continued.

"Yes, please follow me." Connie turned and led them up the stairs.

Rand trailed behind them, keeping his distance, following protocol. Soon enough he'd move to the fore. He admired the way she carried herself like a woman facing battle with confidence enough to win. *But then she doesn't yet know why we've come.*

She led them into a bright updated kitchen at the rear of the apartment. "Annie, it's the police." With effort, she muted the quaver in her voice.

Rand liked her effort to sound normal. Sometimes, the hysteria of friends and relatives made matters worse.

Mrs. Nielsen, looking like a college coed, rose. She stared at the two of them with wide horrified eyes. "Troy…" She wobbled.

Rand took the wife by both arms. "Get her a glass of water please, Ms. Oberlin." He lowered the wife into the nearest chair and pushed her head down to her knees, resting his hand on her back.

The friend did as he requested and brought him the glass of water. "You can call me Connie," she murmured.

He nodded and then turned to the wife. "Most people call me O'Neill, ma'am. I'm Rand O'Neill, a detective from Taperville." Lifting Annie's chin, he put the rim of the glass to the her lips. "Please try to take a sip. It will steady you."

The woman moaned, but obeyed. "Where's Troy? Did you find…" she began in a weak voice.

"Mommy! Mommy!" Little-boy voices came from the front of the flat.

Connie moved as though to go but a hand on her arm stopped her.

"I'll see to them." The other woman in the kitchen hurried out of the room.

"That's Annie's sister," Connie answered his un-asked question.

Rand met her gaze. Her brown eyes held his without flinching. She obviously was the stronger of the two women before him, but then she wasn't the wife.

"Why don't we all sit down?" Hess suggested in a manner that did not allow for any objection.

Rand took the chair beside Mrs. Nielsen while Connie sat down on the opposite side of her. He slipped his supportive hand from the wife's back. He stretched his legs under the table while he waited, ready to judge reactions.

Hess backed into the chair across the table from them. "I'm officer William Hess of the local precinct. You called us earlier to report a possible missing person. And O'Neill's suburban department notified us when they located and identified Troy Nielsen's pickup truck abandoned on a road in Taperville."

Connie gasped. The wife moaned.

"I had worked late. I was driving home." Rand kept his voice low, matter-of-fact. "I was almost to my place when I came up to the pickup—doors wide open and half in a ditch—beside the road of the forest preserve. Not a well-traveled or well-lit area."

"The truck was empty? Did he have a flat tire? Why would Troy leave his truck there?" the wife asked, but didn't have the strength to raise her eyes to his.

"I found no sign of violence, ma'am. But not finding the registration and the fact that the vehicle plates were missing made me suspicious, so I called in the VIN number."

"Why did it take you so long to contact us then?" Connie demanded. "How long does it take to run a vehicle registration?"

O'Neill gave her a measured glance. This wasn't the usual question he got. "Computers were down for a time. It took us a few hours to run down who the owner was, using the vehicle's identification number."

"Troy abandoned his pickup?" Annie Nielsen whimpered, straightening up. "Why would he take off the plates?"

"I don't know, Mrs. Nielsen. As I said, I found no evidence of foul play, but the pickup wasn't just abandoned. Can you think of any reason your husband would remove all evidence of ownership?" *It*

*makes this look very suspicious. Honest men don't
remove identification from their vehicles.*

The wife shook her head no.

"O'Neill's department," Hess said, proceeding
with his explanation, "contacted our precinct because your husband resides here and of course, we'd
had your earlier call. So I agreed to come with
O'Neill so he could question you. He needs enough
information to decide if Mr. Nielsen has been a victim of foul play or if he has…disappeared for some
unknown, but non-threatening reason."

"There isn't—there aren't…" Connie fell silent.

Rand expected denial. That was the natural reac-
tion. Even for an evidently strong woman like this.
"It's just too early to know what has happened,"
Rand said in a soothing tone he'd often used.

While making himself comfortable in the hard-
backed chair, he studied Connie. Savvy intelligence
illuminated her eyes. "Nielsen could be anywhere.
We have no evidence but the abandoned pickup."

"Troy didn't stay away from home tonight volun-
tarily," Connie objected. "He would never do anything to cause Annie pain."

Rand gave her a look. *Why are you still taking
the lead?*

"He could be hurt, couldn't he?" the wife asked,
looking up. "Near a forest preserve…people get
waylaid…"

"A search will be started as soon as we get more

information. I know it is upsetting, but odd things happen. People make sudden decisions, change plans, do the unexpected." Rand lifted both hands.

He took the water glass from the wife's shaking fingers and set it on the table. He glanced to Connie. "Is Mrs. Nielsen a tea or coffee drinker?"

"Tea," Connie said, obviously getting his drift. "I'll put the kettle on." She moved to the stove and picked up the kettle.

As Rand rode the waves and curls of emotion eddying around him, he lowered his tone, keeping his focus on gaining information as painlessly and unobtrusively as possible. "I always think a cup of something warm helps, Mrs. Nielsen."

"Call me Annie. Please." She leaned against the back of the chair. "I can't think. I can't understand...why would Troy...something must have happened..."

"Can you tell me why Troy's truck would be in Taperville, so far from home?" Rand faced Annie but tracked the friend also. She set the full kettle on the burner and ignited blue flames under it. She turned, resting her slender figure against the counter.

"He's working on a construction site there—a new office complex near the tollway." Annie broke down again.

"You can do this," Connie urged her.

Annie shook her head. "Please," she appealed to

Rand. "Ask Connie…she's a lawyer. She'll know what you need…I can't…" Her voice failed.

A lawyer. Again, Rand reached out to soothe Annie, resting a hand lightly on her shoulder. "All right. I'll ask Connie the questions. But if you think she hasn't given me all I need to know, will you chime in?"

Annie choked back tears and nodded, barely meeting his eyes.

Looking uneasy, Connie sat down. "What do you need to know, Mr. O'Neill?"

"Please call me O'Neill. Everyone does," he said. He waited until she met his gaze. She didn't like what was going on, but who would? "When was Troy expected home?" He looked down at his open notebook.

She cleared her throat. "Annie and her family were giving me a party tonight. Troy was expected home early from work." She pursed her lips. "I was late myself—Friday night traffic."

Rand nodded encouragingly. "What was the party for?"

"I just passed my bar exam and my first week of work at my first law firm." Connie looked away. The kettle whistled and she escaped his scrutiny to make the tea.

"I have most of Mr. Nielsen's routine information already from the DOT records." Rand shifted in his chair. It creaked and sounded loud in the tense room.

"So I'm going to ask some questions," he continued in his routine steady tone while digging into his
jacket pocket, "which may upset you and Mrs. Nielsen but which are necessary. If I'm going to find out
why Nielsen didn't come home tonight, I need to get
a clear picture of him and what's going on in his life."

"But what caused this might have nothing to do
with him," Connie spoke up. "He might just have
been in the wrong place at the wrong time."

"That's true, but I have to start somewhere. You
see that, don't you?"

Annie nodded, accepting a white handkerchief
from his pocket.

Bringing the teapot to the table, Connie placed
herbal tea bags into it to steep and poured in steam-
ing water. The fragrance of the orange blossom tea
wafted up from the pot. She ignored him throughout
the process.

"Very well," Connie finally conceded. "I'll tell
you what I can."

"With your law background, you should be able
to give me the type of information I need. How close
are you to Mr. and Mrs. Nielsen?"

"I grew up next door." Connie's voice thickened
with emotion. "And I'm in contact with Annie on a
weekly basis by phone."

"I see." Rand jotted down a note. "How long has
Troy been working in Taperville?"

"I think he started this project in midwinter."

Rising, Connie got down four mugs from hooks beneath the cupboard. She looked over her shoulder, her face in shadow. "Isn't that right, Annie?"

Annie made a sound of assent.

"Is he self-employed or what?" Rand asked, quelling the urge to stare at Connie.

"No." Connie shivered visibly. "He's a journeyman in the carpenter's union. The company he works for is owned by Troy's uncle Lou, Lou Rossi of Rossi Construction."

She was doing a good job at giving information. Rand nodded, jotting down the name, keeping his eyes down so the flow would continue.

"Lou's out looking for Troy now. When Troy didn't show up tonight, he couldn't think of any reason why Troy would have been delayed." Connie voice quavered.

"He and his uncle are close then?" Rand looked up.

Annie mumbled, "Yes."

"Very close. Lou has no children of his own." Connie's voice grew steadier. "Uncle Lou is kind of an unofficial uncle to all of us—Gracie, Annie and me. We grew up with him visiting the neighborhood often to see Troy. He helped me find a position with my present law firm."

"And your firm is?" Rand caught her eye.

"Mulvaney, Vincent and Grove."

"That's in Taperville, too." His gaze lingered on

her. *And not all of their clients are as squeaky-clean as they probably want you to believe.*

"Yes, Uncle Lou is one of their important clients and you know how much new construction there's been in Taperville in the past ten years." Connie stopped. "That's the connection."

Rand finally broke eye contact with her. What was it about this woman that drew his attention? Was she hiding something? "This is all very straightforward. If there was to be a family party tonight, I would think that your husband would make every effort to arrive on time. I think we better get a search of the area of the forest preserve started now." He snapped open his cell phone and punched in some numbers.

While he gave this information to his department, Connie filled the mugs and gave the first one to Annie. When he hung up, she said, "Thanks."

Annie took a cautious sip and then wept quietly into his handkerchief.

"Can either of you," Rand asked after shutting his phone, "think of any reason Mr. Nielsen would have for not showing up tonight?"

"No," Connie said flatly. "I've known Troy all my life. This is not like him."

Rand had heard this phrase many times before and many times subsequent evidence had proved it false. But he held his peace. Unless he was very mistaken, they'd find out soon enough that—unfortunately— every man had his secrets, his vices.

"I would think that finding his truck abandoned," Connie insisted, "would lead to the conclusion that...*something* prevented him from arriving home tonight, that this isn't just a fluke."

Rand met her challenge with a nod. "Yes, but I have to make sure I've gathered all possible information. I'm sure you understand that, counselor." He watched as a few dark strands of her hair slipped from the ponytail at her nape.

Looking troubled, Connie handed him and the other officer mugs. Lifting graceful arms behind her head, she tightened the band around her ponytail and then ran her fingers through it.

Rand swallowed and then touched Annie's arm again. "My goal is to find your husband and bring him home safe and sound, Mrs. Nielsen."

Annie nodded, his handkerchief still pressed to her mouth.

"Now, has anything been bothering your husband?" Rand's pen hovered over his pad, awaiting her answer.

Connie's heart raced. Would this detective get the wrong impression?

"No, not recently." Annie sniffled.

"Had anything upset him in the past year?" Rand asked.

Connie watched O'Neill. He'd been so gentle with Annie thus far. Even as he'd questioned them, his low voice had held understanding, comfort.

Annie wiped her eyes. "I started back to school last summer. Troy didn't take it well…to begin with. He wanted me to have another child first. We have twin boys. They're five now."

"You're pretty young to have sons almost ready for school." Rand smiled at Annie.

Connie appreciated his attempt to bolster Annie. Her first impression of him had been of a man without sensitivity. He'd looked so hard downstairs.

Annie twisted the damp handkerchief around her fingers. "Troy and I married right after I graduated high school. The twins were a surprise though. So I delayed going on to college. But when they were four last year, I decided it was time for me to start taking classes—just as Troy and I agreed before we were married."

"But Troy had changed his mind?" Rand prompted and set his mug on the table.

Connie let herself down into her chair again. The reference to last summer's crisis was draining her in some way. She lowered her eyes and found herself studying the detective's hands—so masculine and capable looking.

"It wasn't a big deal." Annie stopped mangling the handkerchief. "It just took us a few months to work through. We went to counseling and we've been closer than ever since."

Connie felt herself drawn to O'Neill, waiting for his plan of action in this awful situation.

"That's why I know something happened to him." Tears flooded Annie's eyes anew. "This just isn't like him. I mean, he has buddies from high school and from work and the union. And he'll go out with them a couple times a month. But he always lets me know well in advance and he never stays out past eleven or twelve. He works long hours at a physically demanding job and we've got the twins. He needs his sleep. And he would never blow off a family obligation." Annie pressed her fist against her mouth, smothering a sob.

Rand took a sip of the herbal tea.

Over the rim of his mug, Connie's gaze met his and was returned steadily. She dared him to argue with Annie's assessment of her marriage.

"How will you find him?" Annie asked, her fist still covering her mouth, holding back her fear.

"The forest preserve will be searched. I'll keep you abreast of what we find," Rand explained gently. "I'd like the names and phone numbers of those friends of his. And we'll wait to see if you get a ransom note or a call from your husband explaining some bizarre occurrence that none of us could have guessed at."

"What kind of occurrence?" Connie pressed him. *I can't think of one that would explain Troy's disappearance, Detective O'Neill.*

"I have no way of knowing at this point." His cell phone rang and he answered it. Within moments, he turned to Annie. "Can either of you tell me why a smear of dried blood would be found on the floor of the pickup?"

"Blood?" Annie gasped and Connie froze in place.

Chapter Two

Connie had anticipated the usual buzz she got from meeting a new challenge head-on, but in vain. On this Monday morning, she stood like an empty suit behind her imposing mahogany desk. A weekend spent worrying about Troy and the blood in his pickup and comforting Annie had sucked the strength and hope out of Connie. Regardless, she shook hands with her first defendant in her first case. She had a job to do.

"I didn't know I was getting such a classy lady as my lawyer." Floyd Sanders, a pale man in his fifties with thinning hair, began by saying exactly the wrong thing to her. He compounded his mistake by holding her hand a bit longer than he should.

Connie smiled back, but secretly wished she could put him in his place. Subtly chauvinistic compliments always put up her hackles. She decided to overlook it...*this* time. "Let's get right to business." She gestured for him to take the chair on the other side of her desk.

He sat down and spent nearly half a minute getting comfortable in the wide leather chair.

Connie's minor had been psychology and she found herself studying her first defendant's obviously nervous body language as well as his shuttered expression. Neither bolstered her spirits.

Her mind wandered. O'Neill's arresting face fluttered through her mind. Did she trust him to find Troy? The search of the forest preserve had come up with no clue or trace of Troy. Where was he this morning—three days after his disappearance? Apparently since there was no evidence that Troy had met with foul play and no ransom note had been received, Detective O'Neill still hadn't concluded whether Troy was a victim or a husband who'd decided to abandon his family. But anyone acquainted with Troy knew he would never leave Annie.

She forced her mind back to the present. "Now, Mr. Sanders, your warehouse at 280 Depot Street in the old downtown section of Taperville was completely destroyed by fire over a month ago, is that right?"

"Yes, it was. Lost a new shipment of pressure-treated lumber in the fire, too." He licked his wide, loose lips.

The image of Annie's bereft face intruded again,

sparking self-reproach. O'Neill's voice echoed in her mind: "Any reason for blood?" Connie glanced down at the state fire marshal's report, blocking out these memories. The facts in the report about the Sanders's fire were damning, to say the least. "Do you have any idea why the fire marshal decided that your fire was suspicious?"

"No, I don't." Floyd Sanders slid forward. His elbows rested on the chair arms and he clasped his hands in front of his mouth. "That's what you're going to have to prove was wrong. They don't know what they're talking about."

Connie nodded without enthusiasm. "I will do my best for you." *I was so excited about this and now—why don't I have a good feeling about it?*

She turned her eyes full force on her client, trying to penetrate the mask he was hiding behind. "I'll need all the information you can give me about the fire. Where were you when the fire alarm went off at—" she checked the report for the time of the alarm "—two-forty a.m. on May third of this year?"

"I was home in bed." He slid back in his seat. "Where would an honest man be?" He stared at his hands clasped in front of him. "It was a Wednesday night." He swore about the lousy police. "Some people work for a living." He glared at her as if she were responsible for the accusation of arson against him.

Floyd Sanders was right. People like Troy worked for a living. And where was Troy, an honest man—

a faithful husband—who should have come home as usual on Friday night?

Pushing away her unruly thoughts, she mouthed a few soothing, yet non-committal words to her client. "Now you also had just increased your insurance coverage on this particular warehouse—"

"Of course I had." He sat up straighter. "Real estate around here is leaping up in price and I knew I'd be handling more lumber at that location. Are you aware of how much the price of building lumber has jumped just in the past six months?"

Again, Connie accepted what her client said and moved on. "I've spent a lot of time studying the fire marshal's report, but I'd like to tour the warehouse myself. Would that be possible?"

"Sure." He gave her a sly glance. "You're a hot dog, huh?"

Connie lifted one eyebrow.

"Want to see everything for yourself and show what you can do, right?" He grinned in a manner she found unpleasant.

"I'm always thorough." *That's why I can't accept three days with no progress on finding Troy. What is O'Neill thinking? Or more important, what is he doing?*

Floyd Sanders adjusted the crease on his slacks. "Good. I like thorough."

She would try to visit the burned-out warehouse on the following day or as soon as she could work it in. He agreed to leave word with the security man that she was to be admitted to the burn site whenever she appeared. Her stomach suffering the weight of some reaction she didn't want to probe, she proceeded. "And you realize that your insurance company has made its own report—one that had a lot to do with your fire being termed as arson?"

"That's right. But it's all politics." He threw up his hands. "This used to be a small town when I first started out. Local businesses were valued. Now all these new executive complexes and new businesses and malls. Taperville isn't the same place. I used to be like this—" Sanders put his two forefingers together "—with the former fire chief. Now?" He shrugged.

"I see." *She did and she didn't like what she saw. Why did I get this case? Because no one else wanted to touch it?*

She rose to shake hands and put an end to this revealing and unsettling interview. Her client leered at her, used both his hands to cover her one and then left.

She stood rooted to the spot. The sounds of telephones ringing in other offices and voices of colleagues and clients walking together to the nearby elevator flowed around her. Evidently she'd drawn the short straw and had been saddled with a doomed case and client. One of the senior legal assistants, Maureen—with salt and pepper hair and a still trim figure—walked by and gave a little wave. Connie responded in kind. On her first day with the firm, Maureen had been pointed out to Connie as the office gossip. But Connie had seen no evidence of this as yet. When Maureen moved out of sight, Connie sank into her leather chair and closed her eyes.

Doom had been her mood since Friday night and it had lingered all weekend. She'd spent every day of the weekend at Annie's. She'd only gone to her Taperville condo to grab a few hours sleep, shower and change clothes. The whole family—Uncle Lou, Gracie and her husband and Annie's dad Mike and his new wife plus Patience and her husband—had also hovered around Annie and her sons, not leaving them alone in their stunned grief. Lou had insisted that he'd continue to pay Annie Troy's regular wages until Troy was found. The bluff man had been devastated and not good at hiding it.

It had been difficult to hide the extent of her own heartache. Troy had been her friend and then in high school, her first sweetheart. An unspecified fear clutched her. What could have happened to him?

Connie stiffened her spine. *I can't sit here and wallow. I've got to do something. But what?*

O'Neill's angular face came to mind again. She'd hated hearing Annie telling him very personal facts about Troy. Connie knew in her head that this was the way it was done. But her heart objected to having a stranger dipping his hands into Troy and

Annie's life. Still, O'Neill was involved in their lives now. And he had been kind.

She glanced at the clock. Only an hour before lunch break. After going over the fire marshal's report again, she could stop by the police department to check on some facts about her case and then drop in on O'Neill. *It might be a transparent ploy, but it's all I can come up with now.*

Seeing Connie striding toward his windowed office at the police department didn't surprise Rand. In that first interview with Annie Nielsen early on Saturday morning, he'd noted Connie's take-charge personality. Ms. Constance Oberlin didn't take things lying down.

So her appearance here on Monday morning right before lunch didn't throw him. What startled him, however, was his marked physical reaction to seeing her. Some switch inside him had been flipped and a restless energy surged through him.

He rose to meet her. "Ms. Oberlin."

She gave him a barely polite smile. "You remembered my name."

I remembered more than that. He pictured her as she moved quietly around the Nielsen kitchen Friday night—unassuming but a magnet to him. This admission cost him. This attractive brunette came in a very stylish package—nice enough to gain even his attention. But did her charm, her quality, go all the way through or was it just skin-deep?

"Your name's in my report, Ms. Oberlin," he said in a casual tone. "If I type something down, I usually remember it. Please sit down." *Why are you here? Is there something you think I need to know but couldn't say in front of the missing man's family?* "Do you have any information for me?"

She sat on the edge of the chair. "Please call me Connie," she reminded him. "I was hoping *you* would have something for me."

"You believe in instant results like on TV? Crime solved in less than an hour?" Rand didn't attempt to curb the sarcasm in his voice.

"No." She squirmed, trying to make herself comfortable? Or trying to avoid his eyes? "It's just… Troy's missing. He may be in danger or lying somewhere hurt." Her carefully controlled voice quivered on "danger." Natural or a ploy to grab his sympathy?

She spoke innocent, seemingly sincere words. He was sorry for her. But he steeled himself to it.

The reality was that violence or crime had entered her existence and that was unchangeable. No matter what had happened to her friend, what he uncovered about Nielsen, once cruelty entered a life, things were never the same—ever.

"I think," Connie went on, heedless, "in such a case, I wouldn't be a very good friend if I were content to let the matter slide, do you?"

"The matter isn't sliding." He tried not to take offense. *I'm looking for him. Whether it looks like it to you or not.* Missing persons cases were the ones he worked on the hardest. Always. But she didn't need to know why. And he didn't need to tell her.

He leaned toward her. Catching a hint of her spicy scent, he tightened his control over himself. *She's involved in the case. She's a source. Ignore everything else.* "I'm following the evidence, it's just not leading me to Troy Nielsen at the moment."

"Any more news about the blood on the seat?" Her gaze didn't leave his face.

Sizing me up, Miss Oberlin? That works both ways. From years of experience, he made himself sound matter-of-fact. "Lou Rossi said Troy had injured himself that day, nothing serious. So that may explain why it was there." He felt her penetrating gaze. "But I've sent a blood sample to the lab to have a DNA test done to it, so we can be sure its his blood." What was it about this woman that challenged him, riled him? "But those tests aren't done in a moment."

He rested his shoulders back against the chair. "The blood did test out as the same blood type as Nielsen and it didn't appear to be the result of an attack. At least, not an attack that took place inside the truck. The blood was just a small smear, no spatter pattern or anything."

He went on, "The forest preserve was searched exhaustively. We're still on alert for Nielsen, as is the Chicago P.D. There's been no ransom note and no reason for Nielsen to be a target of kidnapping. Believe me, if there was the slightest evidence of foul play, we'd pursue it to the end. But there isn't any. None."

She nodded, biting her lower lip.

Have you got some details you've withheld out of concern for your friends' privacy? Maybe this conversation could lead somewhere with a little gentle, astute prompting. He lowered his voice. "You said you are a longtime friend of the Nielsens?"

"Yes."

He glanced at the wall clock. "How about a sandwich? My treat?"

She looked surprised at his switching gears. Lunch together would get them in a different, less intimidating setting. And he'd found long ago that people talked more freely to him if they were in a more casual setting and eating food paid for by him.

"Well…" she stalled.

"We're both busy people and we both have to eat. Let's go across the street to the deli." He stood up, forcing her to come to a decision.

Her lips a straight line, she rose. "All right."

He ushered her out of his office and through the department out into bright summer sunshine.

Rand noted with a wry twist the envious glances other officers cast him as they took in the woman beside him. With her glossy hair and stylish outfit, Connie Oberlin was appealing, but more than that,

she projected a persona of competence and sophis-
tication that was palpable. Maybe that accounted for
his continued response to her. Some women just
commanded a reaction.

But he knew how to handle people involved in
cases, how to get what he needed from this woman.
If she had it.

Jim's Deli, rich with the aromas of garlic and
onion, was already busy with people lined up at the
counter. Connie made her choice, Rand gave their
order—two pastrami sandwiches on rye with the
works. They poured their own drinks at the fountain
and then he led Connie over to a booth.

"I'll have to remember this place." She glanced
around. "It smells delicious in here."

Again, he noticed that the woman across from
him was one of the most physically beautiful, certainly the best-dressed, women in the deli. Did she
use clothing as armor? As a way of keeping others
like him at bay? "You'll love the pastrami. In my
opinion, the best in the Chicago area."

"High praise. I look forward to it. Now what did
you bring me here to find out?" She took them back
to their reason for being here together.

"I need to get," he chose his words with care, "a feeling about the relationship between the husband and
wife. Can you tell me about them—not in way it would
appear in a police report? Do you know what I mean?"

She avoided his eyes.

"I'm not asking you to divulge anything you've been told in confidence," he assured her. "I just need to get more information than people are usually willing to say around a stranger."

Her eyes lifted. They were a rich brown and very earnest, almost grave. "I wouldn't tell you," she said with a trace of grit, "anything I'd heard in confidence."

"I don't think you would," he said. This appeared to appease her. He admitted grudgingly to himself that this woman with her steady gaze would speak the truth. *This one doesn't flinch.*

She drew in a long breath and began. "We all grew up in the same neighborhood. Troy and I were in the same class. We dated in our freshman and sophomore years in high school but broke up." She looked at him and a smile lifted one corner of her mouth. "We were more like friends than sweethearts anyway. Then a very pretty redhead moved into our neighborhood." She grinned, though with a bittersweet expression on her face. "Troy dated her for a while, not long. I think Annie was already catching his eye."

"So when did his interest in Annie develop?" Rand prompted, watching her every expression, noting a subtle but very real tension behind her words. Something more than he'd expected from a missing person's friend.

"A few years after we finished high school." Connie focused on a point over his shoulder as though looking into the past. "I think he'd been waiting for her to get old enough. He asked her out when she started high school. Her dad, Mike, didn't like it at first, Gracie wrote me. Gracie and I are the same age, a few years older than Annie, so I was off at college." She sipped her drink. "Troy was already out of school and working for his uncle as a carpenter apprentice. Mike thought he was too old for Annie."

"Ah." Rand took a drag on the straw in his cola.

"But after a while, Mike decided that Troy was a good guy."

"Sounds like a fairy-tale romance," Rand said, concealing his skepticism behind a light tone. "Annie said that they'd had trouble a year ago?" He watched Connie's face, her chin firmed.

"Yes, Annie moved out for a while." She looked at him from under lowered lashes, thick black lashes.

"Moved out?" *Now that's interesting. But not unexpected.*

"Don't jump to any conclusions." She lifted both hands, palms up. "Annie told you that Troy was upset that she had started back to school last summer."

"*But* Mrs. Nielsen…Annie," he objected, pulling out an interesting fact he'd discovered this morning, one he'd been waiting to spring on Connie, "didn't tell me that she had filed for separate maintenance last year."

Stiff silence.

The waitress at the counter shouted out their number. *Bad timing.* It would give this woman time to spin this. Rand hated to, but he got up and left the lady with her thoughts. He returned with two wax-paper-lined baskets of fragrant pastrami on rye sandwiches, each with a large whole kosher dill pickle. He settled back down across from her.

"Annie," Connie said, concern tingeing her voice. "probably didn't say that because it makes their problems last year sound worse than they were."

He weighed her obvious caution. "You understand then how important it is for me to get all the facts, even the unflattering ones?"

She nodded stiffly and continued. "Troy was upset with Annie for leaving him…for not staying to fight out their argument over her going back to school. He told her she couldn't see their boys until she moved back—"

"And she retaliated by serving him with separate maintenance papers." What Connie said sounded plausible. Tit for tat. A too-common operating procedure.

"Yes," Connie admitted. "If she'd consulted me…I was a law student at the time, it might have been handled differently." Connie picked up half of her generous sandwich. "But she didn't want to involve anyone—friend or family—in the dispute." She bit into her sandwich.

"How long were they separated?" He took a bite of his crisp dill pickle.

She finished chewing and wiped her lips with her paper napkin.

Watching her try to eat the juicy, overflowing sandwich like a lady lifted one corner of his mouth in amusement. A spot of mustard on her upper lip had eluded her.

He handed her another napkin. "Right there." His index finger hovered above her small, well-defined mouth. Her skin glowed creamy and smooth in the sunlight flowing through the floor-to-ceiling window beside them.

Stop noticing. He picked up his sandwich to distract himself from her.

She looked chagrined as she wiped the spot away. "I don't know the exact length of time. But it was all over before the fall semester started. After some counseling, Annie and Troy came to an understanding fairly quickly."

He could easily check this out. Again, his gaze was caught by her clear, intelligent eyes. "I wish people would understand that it only makes me more suspicious—rather than less—when they color the facts to make them more…"

"Complimentary?" Connie shrugged. "Isn't that just human nature?"

"Guess so," he agreed. "Anything else you can tell me?" he asked, offhandedly. "Anything that might lead me to someone having a grudge against him or Annie?"

She shook her head. "Troy and Annie aren't rich or powerful or nasty. No one could profit financially from harming them. And they're not the kind of people who bring out the worst in others. Something like this shouldn't be happening to them."

He struggled against the sympathy she engendered in him. He couldn't give into it. How did this woman keep breaching his defenses?

"Hey, bro!" a familiar voice hailed Rand. "Hey." His brother Chuck slid into the booth, bumping Rand over to make room. "Hello, pretty lady. Don't tell me my brother finally got a lunch date."

Chapter Three

"This is a business lunch," Connie said in a starched tone.

The connection between them shattered. Aggravation sputtered through him at his brother's poor timing and sad attempt at humor. *I was gaining her confidence, actually getting somewhere with her.* "Sorry, *Ms. Oberlin*," he said, using her formal title to impress on Chuck that this was indeed business. "This is my brother, Chuck O'Neill. He thinks he's amusing."

"Sorry." Chuck offered her a hand across the table.

"No problem." Connie shook his hand and allowed a small polite smile. "You couldn't have known."

"No, I mean I'm sorry you're not my brother's lunch date," Chuck explained with gusto. "He never—"

"That's enough," Rand cut him off. "So? What do you want?"

Chuck clicked his tongue. "Bad manners, big brother. I'll have you know that tomorrow I'll be Taperville's newest detective."

Rand stared at his brother. "I thought you'd decided to go back to college—"

"No, you convinced yourself that you'd convinced me." Chuck winked at Connie.

Rand scowled at Chuck, his jaw clenched.

"Congratulations, Chuck," Connie said with obvious, yet polite, disinterest.

"Fine. Congratulations," Rand growled. "Now you may leave. Ms. Oberlin and I were discussing a case." He glowered at Chuck.

Connie glanced at her watch. "I've got to be going. I have a one o'clock meeting."

Was that true or was she taking advantage of the interruption so she wouldn't have to continue answering his questions? Rand bumped against his brother, trying to get him out of the way so Rand could head Connie off. Chuck didn't budge an inch.

She edged out of the booth and nudged her basket toward Chuck. "I never touched the other half of my sandwich if you'd like it."

Rand gritted his teeth. By the time he could oust Chuck, she'd be gone. To acknowledge her departure, Rand stiffly lifted himself where he sat. "Thank you for your time, Connie. I'll be calling you soon."

"Thank you for lunch." The pretty young lawyer left with a wave of her hand.

Chuck moved to the other side of the booth and scooped up the remaining half of Connie's sandwich. "Free lunch—great."

Rand glared at his brother. "That wasn't very professional. I was in the midst of interviewing her as a source."

"A source?" Chuck grinned. "She looked like she could be the source of many interesting develop—"

"Don't go there." Rand felt hot under his collar. Not the least from the fact that his brother should have taken his advice about finishing his degree. *He's too young, too green. This job will eat him alive.*

Rand pinned Chuck with his gaze. "She happens to be a new lawyer in town. And I wouldn't go making any sexist remarks in her vicinity. I think she has a long and very accurate memory."

"Okay. Okay." Chuck held up one hand. "*Mea culpa.* What's the case?"

"A close friend of hers disappeared here Friday night." Rand kept his voice even.

"I heard about that." His brother eyed him as though looking for...what? Some weakness, some admission about the past? "Tough one."

Ignoring his brother's scrutiny, Rand shrugged. Missing person cases were always tough for everyone. Not just him. "This case is slippery. I can't get a handle on whether we've got a victim or—"

But Chuck's interest was wandering. He stood up and waved. "Hey, Sheila, over here!"

A young attractive uniformed officer with short red hair approached their booth. "Have room for me? I don't want to take my sandwich back to the department."

"I always have room for you, Sheila," Chuck schmoozed.

Rand stood as the young woman sat down beside Chuck and across from him. He'd finish his sandwich and get back to his computer screen. The Internet provided so many places and ways to look for someone who'd gone AWOL from his life.

"Nice manners, Rand," she commented and then glanced at Chuck. "Why don't *you* learn some?"

Chuck grinned and went on eating.

Rand wasn't fooled. He already knew that Chuck was pursuing Sheila and she was giving him a good run for his money. Rand suddenly felt a hundred years old. Unlike him, maybe Chuck would be one of the few lucky ones. He'd find love and keep it.

Rand switched his thoughts back to the Nielsen case and Connie. He tended to believe her take on the trouble the couple had experienced last year. But what might that separation have led to, if anything? Or was it totally unrelated to Troy's disappearance? *This just doesn't feel like a kidnapping. No ransom note. Troy, where are you and why did you ditch your pretty little wife? Jerk.*

* * *

Four days had crawled by since Connie had interviewed her client in the arson case. Routine legal work, contracts and depositions for other cases had eaten up her time each day.

Each night she'd spent at Annie's, helping out with the twins and generally being there to relieve and support the family. Patience and her husband had had to go back to their home downstate. Annie was putting up a good front especially when the twins were around. Still, Connie's stress level spiked each time she'd walked into Annie's place. And she'd waited to hear from Rand O'Neill in vain. Was no news really good news?

But during office hours, Connie had worked hard to keep her mind on business. Now today, she entered the elevator across from her office in late afternoon. She was finally going to tour the burn site.

One of the partners of the firm, T. R. Grove—a distinguished, well-preserved man in his early sixties—joined her and smiled. "Trying to get off early on Friday?"

Connie returned the smile. "No, I'm off to do some research."

"That's a good excuse." The door opened and he stepped out.

Connie was left with nothing to say. What could she say? Any excuse would sound like just that—an excuse. Grove hadn't struck her as an odd duck when she'd interviewed for the job. *Stop obsessing. He probably was just trying to make small talk.*

But now she almost felt guilty. *I'll just come back to the office after I tour the site and check for messages. That should make the point I wasn't leaving the office early for personal reasons.*

As she drove to the gutted warehouse on yet another very warm day, she tried to control her discouragement over today which was, Grove had reminded her, Friday. Troy had been missing for one week today.

Lord, we've all prayed. Our churches are praying. What's happened to Troy?

O'Neill's mocking voice echoed in her mind— *You believe in instant results? Like on TV?*

The blackened shell of the warehouse loomed at the end of a street near the freight railroad line. Connie parked her car and approached the acrid ruins. Her lack of experience taunted her. She wished she'd been able to find an impartial expert. Reading up on the subject had not given her the confidence she wanted. *What do I think I'll find that the fire marshal missed? What do I know about arson investigations?*

"Well, I'm about to learn, firsthand," she muttered.

"Hey!" a gruff voice hailed her. "This is private property." An older man in a work uniform limped toward her. "And it's dangerous. I was hired to keep everyone out of here."

She took out her driver's license and held it up like a badge. "I'm Mr. Sanders's lawyer, Connie Oberlin."

"Thought you would've come earlier this week." The man studied her license.

"I tried to get here, but things kept coming up." She slipped the ID back into her purse.

"Are you sure you want to get dirty?" The man eyed her business suit. "And it's touchy. Some places aren't too safe."

Motioning him to follow her, she walked to her trunk. She opened it, slipped her purse in and pulled out a package. "I bought this. I should be fine." She ripped open the clear plastic and removed a gauzy white painter's coverall she'd purchased at a hardware store. Everything she'd read had suggested that a fire scene was indeed a dirty crime scene.

"Okay. Have fun, Ms. Mason." The older man walked away with a wave over his head.

At first, she didn't get his calling her by the wrong name and then it clicked. *Ms. Mason as in Perry Mason. At least he didn't call me Della Street.*

Then she slipped her key into a pocket, lifted a flashlight, camera and clipboard from her trunk and slammed it shut. Prepared, she headed into the fray. Before long, she wished she'd brought a nose plug, too. The smell of a fire—one which had included the burning of treated wood—left an indescribable stench.

After reading the marshal's report so many times she felt as though she'd memorized it, she had no trouble in locating the fire's point of origin. Or what the fire marshal had decided was the point of origin—the fuse box.

The fact that the warehouse still had an antiquated fuse box rather than circuit breakers struck Connie as suspicious in itself. *I can't believe Floyd Sanders hadn't brought this up to code. But I don't want to make a big deal out of that, either. It makes him seem more culpable rather than less.* Her spirits lowered.

Switching on the flashlight, she studied the burn marks on what was left of the charred wall around the fuse box. Some wires had obviously been clipped and taken as evidence. That had been in the report. She followed the remaining wires trying to see anything that would give her something that might work to her client's advantage.

Her cell phone rang. She flipped it open. At first, she only heard sobbing at the other end.

Then a quavering voice mumbled, "Connie? It's... Annie."

"Annie, what is it?" Had Annie gotten bad news about Troy? Connie's heart jerked to a faster pace. "What can I do?"

More weeping. "Please...talk...detective. Can't take this...much long-er."

Frustration and dismay shivered through Connie. It had been a week now. They should have heard something from O'Neill by now. "Don't worry, Annie. I'll go right now."

"So worried…can't sleep."

"Is Gracie there with you?" Connie asked.

"No, Sandy."

Sandy was Mike's second wife and a sweet person. Connie was grateful that Annie wasn't alone. "I'll call you after I talk to him."

"Okay." Annie hung up.

Connie turned and headed back to her car.

Jittery, Connie approached the classic 60s brick ranch home on the edge of Taperville, O'Neill's house. His intriguing face came to mind, his dark brows drawn together in a customary frown and his cool gray eyes. His mouth that rarely smiled. She felt like she was approaching a lion's cage and the lion might not have eaten for the day.

But the memory of Annie's weeping on the phone stiffened her resolve. She must pick up something, any little fact, to help Annie get through another night. She pushed the doorbell hard and long and waited, conscious of the heat of late afternoon. Perspiration dotted her upper lip. She took a deep breath. *What's the worst he can do to me?*

O'Neill opened the door and stared at her, betraying no reaction.

"I'm sorry to bother you at home," she stammered, awareness of him splashing over her. He was dressed in cutoffs and a T-shirt. The casual attire made her more abashed at intruding, made him more intimidating rather than less. "I need to talk to you."

"How'd you find me?" He held a spatula like a spear in his hand. He moved not an inch. His brooding presence lapped against her consciousness—insistent, almost menacing.

"I stopped at the department and your brother gave me your address." She shifted on her feet. While talking to Chuck, tracking down Rand hadn't seemed intrusive. She'd been a fool. She was invading his space. And he wasn't a man one wanted to trespass on. Only Annie's need held her in place.

O'Neill had planted himself in her path and his stance warned her away. She gripped her resolve tightly. She glanced downward though her eyes wanted to connect with his. She fought his sway over her. "Chuck said you wouldn't mind."

He let out a rush of air—a sound of irritation. "Come in." But no welcome tinged his voice. He motioned her to enter.

She hesitated at the threshold, feeling that crossing it would be a violation of their limited acquaintance, that she would regret entering this man's private realm. She did already. "No, we can talk out here. I don't want to invade your—"

"Come in," he repeated, a sharper edge to his tone. "I'm cooking and don't want my supper to burn."

The snap in his tone energized her. He wasn't happy, but he'd be more aggravated if she caused the ruin of his meal. With palpable hesitance, she allowed herself to be drawn inside and back to the kitchen. She didn't have a right to be here. *But you are here,* a little voice admonished.

Guilt weighed down her stomach, both over Troy and over crossing a line of professionalism with this detective, of bearding the lion in his den. "I'm sorry to bother you at home and on a Friday night."

A trespasser, she halted by his maple kitchen table. Golden sunshine bathed the bright room, which surprised her. Neat, orderly, in shades of white—it was the antithesis of the grim man standing in its center.

"Annie called me about twenty minutes ago in tears," Connie continued, trying to project the urgency she felt into her tone.

She let her eyes rove over the room. White curtains at the window fluttered with the warm breeze. With her fingers, she lifted the weight of her damp hair off her warm neck. A welcome breath of coolness whispered on her nape. "It's the first time she's asked me to find you…" Finally, she couldn't resist the impulse. She looked into his eyes.

O'Neill ignored her words, but stared at her as though trying to pierce her flesh with his gaze. Then he moved to the stove.

"Have you made any progress in finding Troy?"

Her voice sharpened more, she felt unnerved by his intensity—drawn to it. "I need something to tell her, something that will give her hope." Connie didn't like the final note of desperation that crept into her voice.

His back to her, O'Neill switched off the burner under a frying pan. He didn't turn around. "I don't want to get Mrs. Nielsen's hopes up." His voice was uncompromising steel. "This is proving to be a knotty case."

His forceful aura drew her. She fought it. "But—"

"Do you want me to make up something for you to tell her?" He turned around. His expression was cynical.

"No," she snapped, as irritated with herself for coming as with him. "Just tell me what you've been doing this week. At least, that much would help."

"What I've been doing this week," he parroted. Mocking her? He approached her, slowly as though pacing out a duel. "Tracker dogs combed the forest preserve for him. They picked up *nada*. He's officially been designated as a missing person and all local, state and national databases have been notified. No leads. I put out an APB on him and his plates. No one has seen either. I've run Troy's name through every possible database from every airline to every credit card company."

"Why?" She fought being intimidated by his powerful presence.

He halted right in front of her, only a kitchen chair between them. His gaze bore into her, deep and hot. "To rule out the possibility that Troy has left on his own."

"Why do you persist in believing that Troy has left Annie?" Her hands itched to shake him, get to him, make him take her seriously. "It doesn't make sense. He's *not* like that."

O'Neill studied her silently. She felt his piercing gaze, panning over her, probing her again, making her uneasy, fearful. Why? Did he know something he couldn't tell her? Or did he think she'd been less than candid? She didn't like it. She didn't want anyone doubting her motivations.

Then self-accusation rose in her throat. Had she come here for Annie or for herself? Had her own fear for Troy's safety propelled her? Had Annie's phone call merely provided an excuse for this visit? She half turned from him, giving him only her profile. Did this detective sense the burden she carried, the guilt about caring too much?

"Connie, we've already discussed this." His voice was cool, heavy with disapproval. "I have to follow the routine. That's how an investigation is carried out. By turning over rock after rock until I find a clue. With your law education, I shouldn't have to point this out."

I won't be dismissed with the standard police line. "What routine lines have you pursued?" she insisted.

"I've told you. I've been investigating his credit cards." He gripped the back of the kitchen chair in front of him.

His nearness flowed over her, forcing a physical response that heightened the flush on her cheeks. "You mean whoever is responsible for his disappearance might have stolen and used them?" She'd thought of that.

"Yes," he explained, "or someone who came along, found Nielsen unconscious in his truck and stole his wallet." Only inches and the chair separated them.

"But how would that help you find Troy?" she demanded. She turned, moved closer. Her knees bumped the rim of the chair.

"It would help me as I try to determine if he's a victim or a man who's abandoned his family."

"No!" she exploded. "Troy wouldn't leave Annie." *Leave me.* This unspoken confession left her emotions spinning. She grabbed for the chair back and clutched his hands instead. She squeezed them, trying to squeeze an admission from him. "Isn't it's possible that Troy might have hit his head and suffered a brief loss of memory?"

"True cases of amnesia are rare." His voice was like cold water dashed in her face.

Connie tightened her clasp over his hands, trying to change him, move him. *Lord, I'm all mixed up. This has nothing to do with me except that Annie and the boys need Troy back. I don't matter. Let my conscience prick me if I step beyond that line.* She stared down at the chair, concealing the depth of her reaction from him.

"You think you have to keep pushing so I'll do my job," he accused her.

"You haven't had to watch Annie dying inside." *Me dying....* She held that back, changing it to, "You just don't know how...it feels." *Know how I feel.*

O'Neill didn't move, didn't blink.

She checked herself again, careful not to say something that might betray her secret to him. *I fell in love with Troy when I was fourteen. And God forgive me, I still care about him. But if he's happy with Annie, I'm happy, too.* "Annie and Troy are a match made in heaven," she said, forcing herself to face reality. "They love each other...."

"A match made in heaven?" Rand jerked his hands from under hers. "I didn't think anyone still talked like that."

"Go ahead, make fun." A backlash of resentment laced her voice and she didn't care how he took it. She leaned forward, challenging him. "You *don't* know how it *feels.*"

"I know how Annie feels." He flung the words at her. He swung away from her and jerked open a cupboard.

Connie stared at his back. What did he say that for? "I don't know what you mean." Then an unwelcome thought occurred to her. What was he trying to tell her? Her heart pounded even harder. "You can't mean…you didn't…"

He turned to face her, his face contorted. "Over ten years ago, my wife was kidnapped from a mall parking lot and murdered."

Chapter Four

Rand vibrated with shock at hearing his own words. He stood there stupidly, holding onto a cabinet door. *Why did I tell her that? Why did I just rip myself open in front of this woman?*

Rand closed his eyes, opened them, and tried to recall why he'd opened the cupboard. He couldn't think. His heart pounded as though he'd just made a dash for his life.

"Your wife? I'm so sorry." Connie's voice flowed soft and rich with compassion.

The words set his teeth on edge. That's what everyone said—"I'm so sorry." What else could anyone say?

"It was a long time ago," he dismissed her comment. He'd revealed his secret to this *stranger.* Heat and then cold flashed through him.

Why had he told her? What was it about this

woman that had breached the wall of silence he maintained around the heinous sin that had stolen Cara from him? He drew breath and forced the lid down over the past, shutting it up tight once more. His emotional rush fizzled, leaving him shaken.

"Then you do know how I…" her voice stumbled. "I mean, how *Annie* feels."

He faced her, letting the cupboard door bang shut. "I always take missing persons cases seriously. You can count on it." He didn't like the impassioned note in his voice. This woman was making him feel—feel things that belonged to the past. He groped for the loosened, shredded ends of his self-control.

Her eyes downcast, she pressed her leather shoulder bag closer to her side. "I'm sorry I bothered you at home. I really have no excuse…"

"It's okay." *Please go. I need time alone.* Something twisted inside him. She looked so crushed, defeated. He hadn't meant to do that to her. "Have you eaten?" Again, his mouth was speaking words he didn't want to say. "I was just making myself an omelet."

"No, I…"

I can't send you away looking like that. "Just sit back down." *Stay.* "Why not eat a bite? We'll talk about something…like the Cubs. Or are you a White Sox fan?"

"I'm not much of a sports fan." She took a step back, preparing to leave him.

The more she edged away, the more he wanted her here. *Stay.* "We'll just eat and then you can go. No strings attached." He finally was able to clamp his mouth shut.

"I don't think I can eat anything." She folded her arms in front of herself.

"Something simple will go down easy." *Please stay. I didn't mean to take my past out on you.* "I'll make the omelets and then we'll just sit out on the deck and relax, take a break." The idea of having this lovely woman sitting beside him for a meal, so he wouldn't have to sit alone as usual, arced through him—an aching need, an undreamed-of temptation. He was amazed at how much emotion he could feel or how much he wanted her here. *Stay, please stay.*

She gave him an appraising look, considering his offer.

"No pressure. Just a quick, quiet meal." His unchecked pulse galloped. He awaited her reply.

"All right." She relaxed visibly as though a burden had been lifted. She let her purse slide off her shoulder down to the chair between them, landing with a jingle of keys. "Can I do anything to help?"

"No," he said, able to draw a deep breath again, "just take off that suit jacket and make yourself comfortable."

"Rand!" a familiar voice hailed him through the open windows. Through the back door walked his very pregnant sister, Molly, and her family.

"We didn't know you had company," his brother-in-law Larry said, grinning at him in a way that belied his words. He carried their two-year-old daughter, Alexa.

Surprise shot through Rand. It took only an instant to see Chuck's hand in Molly's sudden appearance. Chuck had sent Connie over, and then Molly to make sure Rand didn't run the pretty lawyer off. *You're dead meat, little brother.*

"We're sorry." Molly, petite and dark-haired like their mother, didn't sound sorry at all and studied Connie intensely.

"Maybe I should go after all." Connie reached for her purse.

"No, my sister and her husband just dropped in to say hi, right?" Rand glared at his sister.

"No," Molly said with a grin. "We've already eaten but we'll sit down with you two. We could use some iced tea if you have it, Rand, and you can introduce us."

Rand continued to glare at Molly, his mouth taut. *I've told you not to keep interfering in my life. I'm content with my life the way it is.* "This is Connie Oberlin." He controlled his tone of voice so Connie wouldn't be insulted. *This isn't her fault.* "She's a lawyer in town," he continued, who was consulting me *about a case.*" He emphasized the last three words. "If she's changed her mind and wants to go home—"

"I'm Molly and my husband's Larry and our little girl is Alexa." His sister captured Connie's hand and shook it. "We live near here and I've been home alone all day without adult conversation. Grown-up talk is just what I need." She waved her hand at Rand. "Go ahead and make those omelets."

Rand sucked in air. *I'm going to get you for this, Molly.*

"Don't bother arguing with her, Rand," Larry said, jiggling the little girl in his arms. "Not when Molly's eight months along. It can be hazardous to a man's health."

Rand gave his sister one last smoldering look and turned to the stove. He cracked and plopped three more eggs into the mixing bowl and began to whisk them.

Molly crossed to his fridge and opened it. "I'll get the drinks," she offered.

Rand tightened control over his reactions, submerging them. Molly could and would pick up on any little clue about how much he'd wanted Connie to stay, and then make a big deal out of it.

"It appears that Rand has iced tea or orange juice," Molly said, as she bent over to look into his sparsely filled fridge. "Or I can make coffee."

"I've had enough coffee today, thanks." Connie stood, still looking disconcerted.

"Don't mind my family," Rand muttered to her. "You've met Chuck so that should have prepared you for Molly."

Connie took it as a joke, fortunately. She smiled.

Within minutes, the five of them were clustered around the picnic table on the rear deck that overlooked the lush green forest preserve on the west edge of town. Where he'd found Troy Nielsen's pickup a week ago.

"This is a lovely setting." Connie looked over her shoulder at the forest.

"Yeah, I'm lucky," Rand conceded. "Bought this fifteen years ago before property values jumped up."

"So what's the case Rand and you are working on?" Molly asked. She was sitting across from Connie and Rand, who sat side by side.

"A friend of mine disappeared near here last week." Connie still looked dazed at being here, sitting beside him.

"Oh, I read about that. Terrible." Molly openly scrutinized Connie. "He must be a really close friend for you to come to Rand's place," she probed further.

"We all grew up together," Connie admitted. "Troy, his wife and her family."

"Where's your family?" Molly asked.

"My parents are gone. I was an only child and I don't have much family left. Just a few distant cousins."

"Rand and I are lucky," Molly said. "We still have our parents and two more sisters and two more brothers."

"A large family." Connie sounded awed.

Molly fixed Rand with a look. "Mom and Dad are expecting you Sunday."

"I'll be there."

"Yes, making one of your limited appearances. For once, please stay longer than a half hour."

Rand made no reply. He sipped his orange juice.

Molly kept up a flow of conversation.

Rand ate his omelet, listening and thinking. A disturbing idea had come to him. Had he dug deep enough for a motive to explain Connie landing on his doorstep tonight? Was a call from Nielsen's wife her true motive?

Finally, Molly took her daughter from Larry, who'd volunteered to help Rand wash up.

Rand stood to retreat inside. "Connie, tell Mrs. Nielsen—Annie—that I'll drop by tomorrow."

"You will?" She eyed him with suspicion.

Rand met her gaze. *Because I want to see if I can get a hint from her why you care so much about another woman's husband that you invaded my home to pursue this case. Were you having an affair with Troy and feel incredibly guilty now?*

His stomach soured at this final thought. "Tell Mrs. Nielsen I like to keep in touch with people in my cases." He walked inside, his brother-in-law following him.

Molly leaned closer to Connie. "This is a first. I don't think Rand's ever before mixed his business with his personal—"

"I'm afraid," Connie rushed to admit, "I forced the issue by dropping by."

"I know. Chuck told us that, too." Molly chuckled. "That's never happened before, either."

"I stepped over the line," Connie said, her voice stiff. "I shouldn't have."

"Don't say that," Molly crooned. "Rand really needs someone to step over the line and often."

Later that evening, Connie perched beside Annie on the over-stuffed sofa in Annie's living room. She wished she had more to tell her. She'd done the best she could, but… Sharing a supper with O'Neill had satisfied her in one way and left her groping for explanations in another. *Why did I stay?*

Connie pushed away the memory of sitting beside him, letting his sister's conversation flow gently over them. *I shouldn't have stayed. I shouldn't have gone there in the first place.*

"I'm sorry I bothered you," Annie apologized, looking down into her own lap.

Connie ached at her friend's somber tone. It reminded her that this wasn't about her. Annie was Troy's wife. She was the one who was truly suffering. *My feelings don't matter.* "I'm sorry," Connie apologized in turn, "I don't have much news to give you."

"I shouldn't have called you like that." Annie closed her eyes and rested her head back on the comfy sofa. "I just fell apart all of a sudden. And I don't know what I thought you could do."

"I did what I could. I talked to the detective on the case." Again, Connie pictured O'Neill at his front door. His black hair swept back from his face, his gray eyes burning into her. Why had he let her in?

"He said he'll come tomorrow to bring you up to speed on what he's been doing." For a moment, Connie almost told Annie what he'd revealed to her about losing his wife.

Though she knew this would paint O'Neill in a sympathetic light to Annie, Connie found she couldn't reveal this intimate fact to anyone, not even Annie. *I'm sure he didn't mean to tell me. Men don't like to reveal themselves like that.* Connie worried her lower lip.

So why did he tell me? Connie forced this disconcerting thought away. *Lord, help me focus on Annie's crisis. There has to be something I haven't thought of that I can do to help find Troy. Where is he? Is he still alive?*

Tears slipping down her face, Annie sat in suffering silence beside her. Waves of Annie's grief and Connie's own anxieties cascaded through her. "Annie," Connie interrupted through the sadness, "Detective O'Neill did a credit card and airline check to see if anyone had been using Troy's cards. Someone might have stolen them from him—"

"He thinks Troy's left me. But Troy wouldn't," Annie insisted in a tired, tear-drenched voice. "He just wouldn't. There wasn't any reason. This just doesn't make sense. I'm so afraid for him, Connie."

Connie had no reply. Silently, she went over the events of last Friday night, trying to pick up some lead, something to find Troy.

Finally, she settled on one fact. Troy had disappeared in Taperville, not Chicago. No one had seen Troy after he'd left work from Uncle Lou's job site. Could Troy's disappearance have something to do with Uncle Lou? She turned the idea over and over in her mind. *What could Uncle Lou have to do with Troy not coming home?*

It was a terrible thought, but it was all she could come up with.

Much later that evening, Rand pounded on an apartment door. It was time to "thank" his brother for sending him Connie Oberlin and for letting Molly know he had.

Chuck opened it. He was shirtless, wearing only cutoffs. He had the nerve to grin broadly. "Hey, bro, come on in."

Rand stepped inside and ran his eyes over the cluttered apartment.

"Okay, okay, welcome to my pigsty. No lectures. I've been studying every possible moment for the past few months for the detective exam."

"You gave Connie Oberlin my home address." Rand faced his brother. "You know you're not supposed to do that."

Chuck flopped down into an armchair that was

topped by several rumpled T-shirts. "I like her and I think she's just right for you."

"Thanks for your opinion. Which, I might add, is completely unwanted and irrelevant. She's involved in a case I'm in charge of. You shouldn't have sent her to my house." His conscience chided him: *So why didn't you keep her outside on the front step? Why did you invite her in and offer her supper?*

"Yeah, I know," Chuck said as he yawned. "But somehow I couldn't just let her go away without any help. She kind of got to me."

Rand made no audible reply. After pushing aside open books, paper and a paper-clip box, he sat down on the cleared space on Chuck's sofa. *She kind of got to me, too. Why did I tell her about Cara?* "Don't do that again."

"But you're always working 24/7—"

"That's my business, my choice."

"Mom worries about you, you know."

Rand stifled a pang of guilt. "No one—least of all our mom—needs to worry about me. I've taken care of myself for a long time."

"She says you've never gotten over Cara."

Rand flamed inside. "Cara's been gone for years." Platitudes flowed over his tongue. "I'm over it. Life goes on."

"Okay." Chuck held up both hands in surrender. "I'll never send a beautiful woman to your door again."

Rand ignored his brother's attempt at humor. "Don't interfere in my life and never again tell Molly any of my business. Got it?"

"Got it."

"What are you doing home on Friday night?" Rand asked, switching the focus off himself.

"Sheila's got duty tonight."

"You're going to have to change your act around Sheila." Rand recalled the scene at the deli earlier in the week, and how Chuck had behaved toward Sheila. "She doesn't take you seriously and why should she? You're always clowning around when you're with her."

"I know what I'm doing." Chuck grinned knowingly. "Ladies like to laugh."

That must be why I don't date. I'm not a barrel of laughs. But he knew he didn't want to date, didn't want to be in the singles fray. *I should be a father by now, with kids in middle school.* He stopped his thoughts. What was going on in his head?

Rand turned back to the topic of Chuck and Sheila. "You're lucky our department permits officers to date. And now that you're a detective, you're going to have to be especially careful. If she really isn't interested in you—"

"Not interested in me?" Chuck squawked, outraged.

"If she really isn't interested in you, you'll have to drop it or get charged with sexual harassment."

Chuck shook his head as if he couldn't believe

what Rand had just said. Chuck sat up and changed the subject. "How's the case coming? Any hope?"

"Not much." Rand stood, preparing to leave. "I haven't even been able to decide whether he's been kidnapped or if he just decided to leave his family. It's a weird case."

"What haven't you followed up that you should have?" Chuck stood also, yawning widely.

Rand considered his brother's question. It was a good one. What hadn't he followed up on?

Uncle Lou. Troy's uncle who owned a huge construction company. Troy had disappeared after leaving Lou's job site. Rand had interviewed Lou and Troy's supervisor and his fellow carpenters. Rand had gotten *nada. But maybe I didn't dig deep enough there, didn't ask the right questions.*

"Well, I wouldn't count Connie out." Chuck followed Rand, who was walking toward the door. "I mean, wait till the case is solved. Just get her number and call her when it's all over. She's got what it takes."

She has what it takes but I don't. Bitter gall surged up into Rand's mouth. Over his shoulder, Rand shot a dark look at his brother, twelve years his junior. Having Chuck messing with his life disturbed his status quo. "Don't do this again, Chuck. If you do, I'll say something to the chief about it. No more meddling. This is a case."

Chuck saluted. "Yes, *sir.*"

Rand strode out the door. He'd lost Cara well over ten years ago. How could Chuck—so young and so naive—understand?

On Saturday morning at Annie's apartment, Connie opened the door for Rand just as she had that first night. He'd expected Annie to answer the bell. Seeing Connie so unexpectedly unleashed a wave of keen awareness of her.

"Hi, I told Annie you'd come, but I didn't expect you to be so early." Connie was dressed in wrinkled yellow shorts and a pale yellow top. She wasn't wearing any makeup and her dark hair was tousled. His fingers flexed, ready to reach out and straighten her hair. He clenched his hands.

Why are you here, Connie? Did you plan this so you would be here when I arrived? He looked with suspicion into her eyes, but to him, her eyes were one of her most attractive, most dangerous features. So he spoke to her chin. "I didn't expect you to be here."

"I spent the night. Annie asked me to. She didn't want to be alone."

"Ah." He nodded, wondering if she was being candid. "I came early to save Mrs. Nielsen worry and then after I've filled her in, we can all go on with Saturday chores and…errands."

"It's very thoughtful of you." Connie backed up and led him up the steep staircase to Annie's flat.

And by coming early I might catch Annie off-

guard and coax some new facts from her. Sometimes he didn't like doing his job. But part of it, a necessary part of it, was shaking information loose. *And that's why I'm here.*

Annie met them at the top of the steps. "Detective O'Neill, thank you for coming."

"Good morning, Mrs. Nielsen."

"Call me Annie, please.

He shook the small hand she offered him; Connie hovered close beside him. "I want to give you a rundown of what I've done. I have been working—"

"I know you have." Annie looked near tears again.

He held out a hand to her again.

She took it and squeezed it once. "Come in. The least I can offer you is a cup of coffee while we talk."

Relieved to find her so composed, he followed Annie as Connie walked beside him toward the kitchen. He controlled the urge to follow Connie with his eyes.

"Connie, will you check on the boys?" Annie asked in a distracted tone. "They should be up by now. They'll miss their Saturday cartoons."

Connie nodded and left his side.

He trailed Annie the rest of the way into the kitchen and, at her gesture, sat down at the table. He slipped out his notebook and opened it. He formulated his first question, but Connie's call interrupted him.

"Annie—" Connie's raised voice came from the living room "—could the boys be downstairs at Gracie's?"

"I suppose so." Annie looked perplexed. "But I don't think so. They'd have awakened me to ask for permission if they were going down."

Connie appeared in the kitchen.

Annie turned to face her. "Did you check my bedroom?"

"They aren't in either of the bedrooms." Standing in the doorway, Connie pressed her hands to each side of the door jamb as though bracing herself.

Annie whirled around and hurried the few steps just beyond the kitchen to the bathroom door. She opened it. Then without a word, she raced down the back steps.

Connie took off after Annie.

At her heels, Rand ran to catch up to Annie. Annie was already pounding on the first floor flat's back door when they caught up with her.

"Annie," Rand started, "What's—"

Her sister, Gracie, in a short white terry-cloth robe cracked open the door. She yawned. "What's up?"

"Are Austin and Andy here?" Annie looked past her sister, straining to see.

Gracie appeared confused. "No, was I supposed to watch them this morning?"

Annie pushed past her. "Austin! Andy!"

No reply came.

The agitated mother turned and rushed past the three of them still gawking at her in the doorway. She ran out the back door. "Austin! Andy!"

But the backyard was empty.

Chapter Five

Down the quiet street of Annie's neighborhood, Rand jogged beside Connie. She'd rushed outside in such a preoccupied rush she hadn't taken time to change or even comb her tousled hair.

They'd left Gracie back at the two-flat, taking care of Annie, who said she had no idea where the boys would have gone. While listening to the women's discussion of possibilities, Rand had already called the local precinct and alerted them that Andy and Austin might have run away. But Connie had insisted on looking first for them in the neighborhood in case the boys had merely strayed.

With each step, he heard her muttering under her breath: "Oh, Lord, please let them be in the park. Let this just be a case of naughty behavior. Please, Lord."

Rand found himself thinking about Molly's little girl. The world was such a dangerous place for little ones alone. He wished he still believed in prayer, still believed God took a personal interest in the lives of human beings. But God lived so far away. Did He care? Did He even notice Annie and her sons losing their husband and father?

At the end of the block, Connie reached a leafy green park, surrounded by an ancient wrought-iron fence, a few seconds before Rand. She ran ahead into the nearly empty park. "Austin! Andy!" She repeated their names over and over.

Rand kept up with her, but his eyes had already told him the twins weren't here. "What next?" he asked.

"Their best friends live on the next block. We can cut through here." She took off, heading toward the back gate of the park.

Connie, you're not thinking. He hustled after her. "Your guess," he called to Connie's back, "that the boys might have come to the park without permission made sense. But wouldn't the friends' mother phone Annie if the twins showed up at her door without their mother?"

She didn't reply.

He hurried forward to head her off. With a burst of speed, he whipped around her and then stopped. He braced his arms against hers.

Connie bumped into him, breathing hard.

"Slow down." He sucked in air. "Let's think this through."

"You're wasting time!" She tried to brush his hands away.

"No, you are." He continued to hold her arms loosely, protectively in his hands. In contrast to her disheveled appearance, she looked and sounded like an avenging angel.

"Connie, we've got to think like the twins. And you know them better than I do. I can see them slipping away to the park on a sunny summer morning. But that obviously wasn't what happened. What would be their motive for leaving their house early on a Saturday morning when they would be missing their weekend cartoons? If we can figure that out, we'll find them."

Connie's restless gaze darted around. She put a hand above her eyes as though her head were paining her. "I can't think."

"Take a deep breath. In and out slowly. Get focused." He waited with his hands still on her arms, supporting her now. The insane urge to take her into his arms to comfort her popped into his mind. He brushed it away savagely. Why did this case keep throwing them together?

"This behavior—this leaving without telling their mother—isn't typical." She wouldn't look at him.

"They've been through a lot this week," Rand said.

"You're right of course. They haven't been behaving normally." Connie grimaced with exasperation.

"So how then can I predict or guess why they left home and their destination?"

"Did they say anything peculiar," he coaxed, "or out of the ordinary last night before bed? When you saw them?"

"No…." her voice faded. He still fought pulling her closer. Giving in, she rested her hands on his arms now. Was she depending on his strength? *Don't depend on me.*

She looked up into his eyes. "They did appear more worried last night than they had this whole week."

"That's what I mean. Think back. Did they do or say anything out of the ordinary?"

Connie frowned, staring at the cracked sidewalk. "The only thing I can think of was that they asked Gracie's husband if he'd take them out in the afternoon like their daddy usually did on Saturdays. It wasn't like them. They looked overeager, agitated somehow. I thought it was just nerves."

This caught Rand's attention. "Where did Troy usually take them on Saturdays?"

"I don't know and I don't think Annie does, either. I don't think Troy took them to the same place twice. They mentioned going to the Oak Street beach once and to get ice cream downtown." She pulled out of his hands, cutting their connection. "I didn't pay a lot of attention. It didn't seem like a big thing. Annie used to spend Saturday afternoon studying so Troy always takes the boys during that time. Trying to show support for her going back to school."

Needing to have something to do with his suddenly empty hands, he rubbed his palms together as he pondered this. He sensed her growing impatience. "Did Jack tell them he'd take them?" he asked.

"No, Jack has a meeting this afternoon with an out-of-town client who was flying out again tonight." She made a move to start walking.

Rand ventured to halt her again with his hand on her arm. "And?"

"But Jack told the twins," she went on, "he'd take them out for ice cream when he got home from his meeting."

Did this mean something or not? Rand couldn't see how, but—

"Rand, we need to go to the friends' house. Please." She stepped around him, but still hesitated.

"Okay, let's do it." He waved her on. "But after you've talked to their mother and alerted a few others in the neighborhood, you need to come back to Annie's with me. In light of Troy's disappearance, unless we are lucky enough to find the twins now, we need to have the precinct put out an Amber Alert on them."

Connie made a sound of despair, pushed past him and began jogging and muttering prayers again.

Rand loped alongside her and considered the possibility that Troy had slipped back home and lured his sons away. But why? Troy had no history of mental instability. Everyone Rand had talked to had agreed that Troy and Annie weren't having serious marital difficulties. No one had hinted that Troy was involved with someone else. Especially not the woman running beside him.

He pushed aside the fact that this satisfied some part of him. It had nothing to do with his investigation. And that's where his mind should focus.

Later, Rand stood in the Nielsen kitchen, Connie beside him. He held the receiver in his hand, talking to the local officer who'd just called him with news.

"A Chicago beat cop found the Nielsen twins and they're on their way home with a patrol officer," said Hess, the local cop who'd come with Rand last Saturday morning to break the news to Annie. "Somehow the twins got on a subway—"

"A subway? What would possess them to get on a subway alone?"

"Beats me. Anyway, a bartender saw them out the window of the sports bar where he was setting up for the day and called them inside. It's not an area where kids should be out alone. He gave them colas and had them sit at the bar. When the beat cop checked in like usual, the bartender turned them over to him."

"Great." With relief, Rand turned to Connie and Annie's family, who were grouped in Gracie's kitchen. "The police found the boys and are bringing them home."

Annie moaned and covered her face with her hands.

"Thank you, Father," Connie breathed, hovering so near Rand that he felt her breath on his ear.

Annie, who'd been silent for the past few hours, began to sob.

Rand thanked Hess.

"You make any headway with your investigation in finding their dad?" Hess asked.

"Following procedure. But I haven't turned up anything concrete."

"Well, when you want them, I've got the name and badge number of the officer that picked them up. You might want to talk to him later and see if he got anything more from the bartender."

"Thanks. I'll do that." Rand hung up.

Annie stood up, gasping. She pressed her hand to her heart. "I can't breathe."

Rand crossed to her and took her wrist in his hand. Her pulse was racing.

Annie pressed her hand harder over her heart. "Chest pains," she gasped.

The door bell rang and Jack went to answer it. The twins walked in followed by two policemen. "Hi, Mommy. We're sorry," Andy said, eyes downcast.

"Yeah, we just went to find Daddy," Austin agreed, chewing his lower lip.

Annie tried to form words, but no sound issued from her. She choked, looking panicky.

"Annie, sit down." Gracie pushed her toward the nearest chair.

Annie began to shake, gasp for air, and then gag.

Rand took her shoulders in his hands and looked into her face. "Mrs. Nielsen?"

She closed her eyes, still shaking.

"I think we need to call a doctor." Rand was all too familiar with the signs of hysteria.

Annie swayed in the chair and began sobbing in low, deep, wrenching gasps.

Later, only Rand, Connie and the twins sat around the Nielsen table. The atmosphere in the room was strained and everyone seemed somehow stunned. Connie picked up a potato chip from Andy's plate. "Come on, guys." Her tense voice didn't even sound like her. "Eat up. You need to give your stomach something to work on."

"Not hungry," Andy said.

"Me, neither," Austin agreed.

Today, Rand had learned how to tell the twins apart—Austin had a mole on his ear; Andy didn't.

Connie looked at the potato chip in her hand as if she wondered how it got there. She dropped it onto her own untouched plate.

Jack and Gracie had taken the hysterical Annie to the nearest emergency room. Rand needed to get the twins to tell him what they'd done before much time elapsed. In their heightened emotional state right now, he might be able to squeeze some fact from them that might give him a lead to follow to their father. This trip of theirs on the subway was too odd, too out of the ordinary, for two little boys. It must have a connection to Troy's disappearance. Had to.

"Is Mommy going to be all right?" Andy asked.

"The doctor gave her a shot, but she'll be home later." Connie bit her lower lip.

"We're sorry," Austin said in a small voice.

"We just wanted to find Daddy," Andy added, kicking his heels against the chair legs.

Why did you think you'd find your daddy at a sports bar in another neighborhood? Rand kept this question to himself, however. Connie wouldn't appreciate it. That much he could predict with accuracy and it nettled him. To her, Troy Nielsen was the perfect father and husband. Why? Why did she have Nielsen on a pedestal?

"Is that all you're going to eat?" Connie asked the twins, sounding as if she didn't really care.

The boys nodded, looking glum.

A half-eaten sandwich sat drying on Rand's plate, too. He didn't have any appetite either for some reason.

"Okay, then it's bath time." Connie rose as though weighed down.

Rand nearly reached out to shore her up but stopped himself in time. Why did she tempt him?

"Uncle Jack said he'd take us out for ice cream,"

Andy muttered, again kicking his heels against the chair legs.

The rhythmic thump-thump depressed Rand.

"That will have to wait," Connie scolded. For a moment, life flooded back into her voice and face.

"We're sorry," the boys said in unison, almost in tears.

He understood Connie's being on edge. Who could blame her? Leaning from his chair, Rand put a hand on a shoulder of each of the boys. Why did they have to learn so young how nasty life was?

"We just want our daddy back." Andy gave a hic-cupping sob and Austin joined him.

Regret clear on her face, Connie knelt and gath-ered Andy into her arms. "I know. I'm sorry for snap-ping at you. This has been a rough week for all of us."

Rand put an arm around Austin's shoulders. Though touched by Connie's tenderness, he needed to get them talking. They might just tell him something they wouldn't say in front of the rest of their family.

"Come on, guys," he said, "you've been really brave so far. You've got to hang on and help out your mom. We're going to find your dad." Rand felt dis-honest saying this. *I have no guarantees that you'll ever see your dad again.* But he couldn't say that. "Now let's go get you ready for your bath."

"You shouldn't have to help." Connie rose slowly, looking at him.

"I'd like to." Over the boys' heads, Rand mouthed, "Let me. They'll act better with a stranger."

Connie nodded. She forced a grin, lifting one corner of her mouth.

"Good." He gazed at her and gave her a wry look. "If I were a real gentleman, while you were bathing them, I'd offer to do the dishes. But I *know* you must love washing dishes."

Connie threw a dishtowel at him, and then swung away immediately. Her shoulders shook and he was sure she was suppressing tears. Once again, he sensed that she was more concerned about this family than she should be. Or was that just his prejudice, his perception? Why did that irritate him? She'd said that Annie and Gracie were like a second family to her. Dissatisfaction still lay in his stomach like hardened cement.

Connie turned back to him, her eyes bright with unshed tears. "While I clear the table," Connie said in a controlled voice, "would you help the boys get their clean undies and pajamas?"

"Sure. We won't be long," he murmured.

He directed Austin and Andy to their bedroom, helped them dig in their dresser drawers for clean Spider-Man underwear and summer pj's. The three of them trooped back through the kitchen to the bath. An old-fashioned white claw-foot tub sat squarely in front of the window.

Connie was there already leaning over turning on the taps.

"Here's our bubble bath." Austin handed him a blue box.

Soon, the boys were in the tub, blowing frothy suds at each other. Connie knelt on the floor beside the tub, shampooing Andy.

Rand gave her a look and mouthed, "Work with me." After receiving her nod, he made himself as comfortable as he could on the stool lid. "So when was the last time," Rand said, keeping his voice nonchalant, "your dad took you to that sports bar?" *And what would your mother think if she knew he'd been taking you to it?*

The boys exchanged looks.

Recalling baths he'd given Chuck when he'd been a kid, Rand scooped up two handfuls of suds and blew them at the twins in turn. "The bartender said that he recognized you." This was a fib or, at least, an overstatement. The barkeep had told the beat cop that the kids had looked familiar. But he couldn't be sure.

He felt Connie's attention on him. But thankfully, she went on helping the boys bathe as if his questions held no interest for her.

"Daddy liked to watch the games on the big screen," Austin admitted, resting back against the tub.

Rand nodded. "I like to do that, too. This must be a nice place."

"Yeah," Andy said, swirling his hands unseen in

the water. "They let you eat all the peanuts and pretzels you want."

"And Daddy bought us soda," Austin added.

Connie seemed to be aware of the delicate operation he was engaged in, in trying to pluck any useful fact from the little ones. She continued bathing the children, but with a soft touch and without breaking into their concentration on him, letting them forget that she was there listening.

"I might want to go there myself." Rand crossed his legs. "How did you two get there?" This had puzzled him. "That was pretty smart of you."

Andy grinned. "We got on the subway all by ourselves."

"Yeah," Austin said with pride. He splashed his palms down through the suds. "We memorized all the stops. Daddy gave us a nickel for every stop we could remember in order—if we could say it before the loudspeaker said it."

"Yeah," Andy agreed, "we saved the money and knew how to get a ticket from the machine."

"We did good." Austin beamed.

"You did." It hadn't hurt that Saturday morning subways were sparsely populated. No motherly type had been there to see the boys and take them in hand.

Connie's worried eyes met Rand's. She gave him a little nod and then began to scrub Andy's back.

Rand scooped up two handfuls of suds and topped each boy's head with some. "But next time, don't do

it without telling your mother first. You scared her."
She doesn't want to lose you, too.

"We won't." The boys spoke in unison in that disconcerting way they had.

"We thought we'd be back before anybody got up." Andy put suds on the end of his nose.

"But we didn't know the bar doesn't open up till later. We never went before lunchtime." Austin imitated his brother and they both blew the bubbles off the other's nose.

Rand nodded with understanding, feeling his way to the next question. "Did your daddy ever meet friends at this place while you guys watched games?"

The twins sobered and exchanged glances. And they eyed Aunt Connie who concentrated on washing the back of Austin's neck, acting as though she wasn't even listening.

"You know I'm trying really hard to find your daddy." Rand didn't look at them directly, but played with the suds. "It might help me if I could talk to more of his friends. Maybe he told somebody where he was going and he just forgot to tell your mom."

The twins communicated worry in a silent conversation of eyes and expressions.

"Maybe we should tell him," Andy said in a small voice.

"We promised Daddy we wouldn't tell Mommy," Austin said in the same tone. Again, the boy glanced at Connie.

"*He's* not Mommy." Andy nodded toward Rand. "And he's trying to find our dad."

"I'm not Mommy, either," Connie said, barely above a whisper. "We need to find your daddy."

A thinking pause. Rand bided his time, batting bubbles above the tub. Connie started scrubbing toes in silence.

"Okay." Andy frowned.

"There was a guy," Austin started.

"He talked mean to Daddy," Andy said, giving a shiver. "He said Daddy better pay up."

"Yeah," Austin added, "they almost had a fight."

"With fists," Andy concluded.

"They did?" Rand tried to sound unconcerned, only mildly interested. Was this a clue or something completely unrelated to Troy's disappearance?

"Yeah, and we didn't like him." Andy shut his eyes and slid under the suds.

"Daddy told us not to tell anybody about this guy. We thought maybe…" Austin held his nose and slid under the suds.

"What?" Rand felt his heart rate speed up. He finally had something to follow up on. Who was this guy? "What did you two think?" He raised his voice so that even underwater they could hear him.

Austin surfaced. "Nothin'."

"What did the guy look like?" Rand ventured.

Austin shrugged. "Just a guy. He didn't look funny or anything."

"Can you think of anything else that might help me? Anything else the man said or anything your dad did?"

Both twins shook their heads.

"Well, you two splash a little longer and then we'll get you to bed." Connie stood up and walked out into the hall. There, she leaned close. "What do you think?" she whispered.

"Too soon to tell," he whispered back. "I'll get in touch with the local precinct in that neighborhood."

His voice snaked through Connie, lifting her from despair. Standing so close to him comforted her in a way she didn't want to analyze. *What an awful, frightening, exhausting day, Lord.* "Should we say anything to Annie?"

"Not yet. Not till I find out it means something."

"Okay."

The boys climbed out of the tub and shook their wet bodies like two little puppies. Connie reached in and grabbed two towels off the towel bar. She handed one to Rand and they both dried down one boy and helped pull on clothing. Performing this homey chore side by side with him went straight to her heart.

"Are you going?" Connie asked when the boys bounded out into the kitchen, begging for chocolate milk. *Please stay.* Then she scolded herself. *Of course, he's leaving now that the boys are home and safe.*

"Do you want me to stay until Gracie and Jack bring their mother home?" Rand sounded merely polite.

"No, no, we'll be fine." Her pulse raced at this mis-
leading phrase. *I'm not fine, not even close.* She made
her voice cheery. "I'm going to read them stories and
maybe pop popcorn. They didn't eat much supper."

"Sounds good."

Again, she heard only courtesy in his voice. *What
more did I expect?* "You've spent all day with us and
I'm sure you didn't plan to," Connie apologized,
wishing he'd insist on staying longer. She didn't feel
quite so desperate when he was with her.

He pushed the door open an inch. "No problem."

"Okay." She turned away to the refrigerator for
milk, but felt his gaze linger on her. *What's going on
with me? I shouldn't want him to stay. He's the detective trying to find Troy. He's not even a friend. But
then why don't I want him to go?*

Nearly a week later on Thursday afternoon, Connie looked up from behind her desk.

"I need to talk to you." T. R. Grove, the senior
partner, leaned over Connie's desk.

For a moment, she felt trapped. And then she
shook off the silly idea. Just because Grove had closed
her office door and just because he was speaking in
a voice only above a whisper didn't mean anything.

"Of course," she responded in a low voice, following his lead. "Have a seat."

Her last comment was superfluous since he'd already seated himself.

"I want to know why you have been spending time this week digging around in Lou Rossi's files here."

She stared at him. *How do you know that?*

"What are you up to?" Grove gave her a keen, assessing look.

Connie tried to decide what line to take, but no thought but the truth came to her. "I'm trying to find some lead to why Troy Nielsen, my friend's husband and Lou's nephew, disappeared after leaving one of Rossi's sites almost two weeks ago."

"Why?"

Connie lifted one open palm. "Because the detective isn't making any progress."

"You're not a police detective," Grove snapped. "You are a junior partner in this firm. You are paid to do the work you are given. Nothing more. This investigation into Rossi will end now."

His crisp authoritarian tone surprised Connie. It was out of character for him. "I'm doing my work. I stay late every—"

"Do you get my point?" He leaned forward, pinning her with a laser-sharp gaze.

"You want me to stop investigating anything at the Rossi site that might have led to Troy being kidnapped," Connie recited like a school child.

"Have the police said they think he was kidnapped?"

"No." She flushed warmly.

"Have they intimated in any way that Rossi is implicated?"

"No," she repeated.

"Leave this matter to the police." Grove stood. "And concentrate on your prescribed duties. Will we have to have another conversation about this?"

"No." Her face blazed now.

"Good." Grove left without looking back. The door clicked shut behind him.

The interview left her shaking like a rubber band some unseen hand was still snapping. She pushed her chair back from her desk and rose. She needed a cup of coffee and a few minutes to figure out what had just happened.

In the empty break room, she poured herself her what, ninth cup of coffee for the day? Or was it the tenth? Maybe caffeine was responsible for her jitters.

Maureen, one of the firm's paralegals, slipped inside. She closed the door behind her. "I tried to cover for you," the middle-aged woman said softly.

"What are you talking about, Maureen?" Connie kept her tone discouragingly cool.

"I just saw Grove leave your office. He looked angry. I tried to cover for you, but it didn't work."

"Cover for me?" Connie wondered what motivated Maureen, what the woman knew. "Why?"

"Grove handles all Rossi work. His aide noticed you were asking for the Rossi Company files and other ones that have to do with Lou Rossi's business public and private. And he mentioned it to Grove this morning."

The revelation made Connie feel like she should start looking over her shoulder. Why would Grove's aide take the time to notice what she was doing? And why would he think it worth the effort to tell Grove? "I don't know what you're talking about," Connie said in a quelling tone, sorry she hadn't put Maureen in her place immediately.

"I'm trying to help you. This office is like a little kingdom. You're old enough to get that. Nobody wants other members of the firm treading on their territory."

Obviously as good an explanation for Grove's tantrum as any. "Again, I don't know what you're referring to," Connie reiterated.

Maureen pursed her lips.

Connie eyed Maureen and then cleared her throat. *What don't I know about Lou Rossi that Grove doesn't want me to find out?* But Connie refused to ask this woman. To do so wouldn't be professional.

"I've got work to do." Connie dismissed Maureen and turned toward the door. But from the corner of her eye, she caught Maureen's look of concern.

"I'm just trying to help you avoid some pitfalls. There are some connections that our clients have that skate along the edge, if you know what I mean?"

Connie opened the door, but froze with her hand on the knob. *What?*

"And a word to the wise, you won't get any thanks from the senior partners for making friends with a police detective."

Maureen gave her a sad smile and left.

Connie didn't move for several seconds. She felt exposed as if everyone in the office had been watching her. Finally, she forced herself back to her office, weighing Maureen's motives and advice.

Late Thursday night, Rand hunched over a stale drink at the murky sports bar where the twins had turned up last Saturday morning and tried not to look like a cop. Cigarette and cheap cigar smoke fouled the air around him and a night baseball game blared from the large TV at the end of the bar.

This was his third visit to the bar this week and he finally felt like he was at the point where he'd sized up some of the other regulars. And that they had become comfortable enough around him to ignore him. No one gave him a second glance.

Rand took his time with his nonalcoholic beer. He'd had to keep a cool head while making sure he looked like he belonged in this smoky bar. So someone—a man who'd threatened Troy—might show his hand.

It was a long shot but it was all Rand had now. The sports bar was like so many others. Primarily men in work clothes or jeans, and some business casual— talking loudly, buying drinks, yelling at the players on the screen.

Then Rand had noticed a man in nondescript jeans and gray T-shirt who had been making his way through the crowded bar since Rand had seen him enter an hour ago. It wasn't the first time this man had appeared here. He'd seen him there on the previous two occasions. But a person had to be watching to see what the man was doing.

Rand stared at the screen, but out of the corner of his eye, he kept track of him. *He's good.*

A question formed itself in Rand's mind. Had Troy Nielsen frequented this bar because of its questionable ambiance, the big-screen TV or because of this sheetmaker?

Chapter Six

On Friday afternoon, Connie found herself in front of Rand O'Neill's desk, in spite of her better sense. Her stomach burned. Lunch hadn't settled well.

Papers littered his desk and he was on the phone. After a brief assessing look, he motioned for her to take the seat beside his desk. He began easing his conversation to an end. He hung up and looked at her again in that measuring way he had. "What can I do for you?" His voice was cool and said, "Don't get too close."

"I'm sorry to interrupt you," she mumbled. *What did I come here for anyway? He isn't exactly comfort central.*

"How are Annie and the twins?" he asked.

"As good as can be expected." Maybe she'd come because he alone in Taperville understood what was upsetting her—though he didn't possess the power to change her worry over Troy and Annie. She shrugged away the longing for this man's sympathy. He had none to offer. But he'd revealed the reason why—he'd lost someone, too.

"I haven't contacted Annie this week," O'Neill said.

"We'll get through another weekend," she commented, still thinking about his tragic loss. After Annie and Gracie's mother had died, her dad had told them: "It isn't what life throws at you. It's how you handle it."

Obviously, O'Neill had dealt with losing his wife by shutting down parts of his life. If Troy were never found, how would Connie respond to that awful truth? For the first time, she consciously contemplated that Troy might be found dead, that Annie might be left a widow or just a deserted wife. *No!*

"I have no progress to report to Annie," he continued, his dour tone making Connie cringe.

I have something to report. I think Lou might have unsavory friends or business associates. And that this might have something to do with Troy's disappearance. She couldn't bring herself to voice these words.

Not Uncle Lou. Not the man who'd been her unofficial uncle for years. *Maureen couldn't have known anything. Saying that Lou skated along the edge. Trying to sound important. She should take up a career writing for tabloids.* But Connie couldn't make herself believe her own words.

"Is there anything wrong?" O'Neill asked, his eyes still analyzing her.

"Nothing," she lied as she contemplated whether or not Troy might have had to flee for some reason. Could that explain his disappearance? Had he seen something he shouldn't? Was he hiding because he'd discovered something shady about Lou? *No, I can't believe that.*

"Did you have anything you wanted to tell me?" He leaned forward. The office sounds—phones ringing, some voices loud above a constant murmur, footsteps on institutional linoleum—surrounded their little island.

She found herself gazing into Rand's gray eyes. He was drawing her in, making her want to pour out her fears to him.

"Do you know Floyd Sanders?" Connie blurted out, forcing them, the conversation away from Troy.

O'Neill looked at her. "Let me think."

"Forget it. I shouldn't have brought that up." She edged forward, feeling like an idiot. *What am I doing? I can't violate client confidentiality. Why does this man tempt me to come to him for help? He can't help me.*

He tightened his jaw and then rose. "I'm due for a break. Why don't we take a little walk? There's a park behind the courthouse."

Yes, let's get out of here. It will make it easier to get away from you. Without comment, she rose and let him lead her outside into the balmy July day. The blue sky and the bright sunshine should have lifted her spirits but didn't.

Rand said nothing and she was grateful. Under no circumstances could she tell him about her suspicions about Uncle Lou or about the prospects for her dismal case.

Finally, when they were alone under a spreading oak, he asked point-blank, "What's bothering you that you don't want me to know?"

I started this. She blinked sudden tears away. "Your sympathy is touching," she said sarcastically. "It's just the usual garbage. Nothing exciting."

Rand gave an unamused laugh. "I get a lot of that myself." He closed his mouth. Silence could be a powerful tool. It made people nervous and more likely to blurt out the truth. *People always let you know what's bothering them, what they'd rather die than let you know.*

"I haven't taken time to take a walk through this park," she said as if they'd just been introduced at a formal garden party. "I've only seen it through the courthouse windows a few times. I didn't realize it had such a variety of flowers."

Come on, Connie. You know you didn't stop by my office to talk about flowers. What's bugging you? But knowing her, it had to do with Troy's disappearance. He experienced a familiar burning in the pit of his stomach.

Outwardly, he agreed with her garden party comment but added nothing. He bided his time, hoping she'd fill in the yawning silence. He hated using his usual tactics on her. She wasn't like everyone else. His inner critic snapped, "That's just an illusion. Everyone is like everyone else."

"Troy's been gone two weeks now." She paused and chanced a look up at him.

Now it'll come. He didn't know whether this pleased him or not.

"Do you think you have made any progress? Did you find out anything at that bar the boys went to?"

Still fencing with me? Rand inhaled deeply. "You'll do well as a lawyer, Ms. Oberlin."

"Why do you say that?" She glanced away.

"You don't give anything away."

"Well," she sparred with him, "you're quite the detective if you've figured that out."

He didn't bother to reply. Each of them had hoped for some information. Then he pictured himself sitting at that bar every few nights over the past week. What would happen if he told her about that? Easy, she'd be at the sports bar that very night, asking everyone there questions about Troy.

The charged silence between them stretched longer, longer. This time, standing with her feet planted and arms crossed, she waited him out, remaining still long enough to make him fill the silence.

He gave a grudging grin at her unlooked-for resistance. "I visited the sports bar, but I haven't discovered anything specifically about Troy." *It's just made me even more suspicious of the man.* "So I've just continued down the list of identifiers for missing persons." He hardened his voice, distancing himself from her, knowing she'd hate every word he said. "No action on his social security card—Troy hasn't taken a job anywhere else. No action on his credit cards—he hasn't checked into a hotel or charged anything. No reservation made—he hasn't flown anywhere. Unless he hopped a freight train or a bus, he's still in the Chicago area."

She didn't like what she heard—he saw it kindle in her eyes, but she didn't retort.

Again, Rand waited, hoping for a hint of a clue. Anything.

"I guess I should just get back to work." Her tone was flat, colorless and totally unlike her.

She was about to slip through his fingers again. *Don't leave—yet.* He took her elbow in his hand. "You came to me for some reason. What is it?"

She chewed her lower lip, staring pointedly away from his eyes.

He pulled out the card he knew would get a response. "Would it help me find Annie's husband?"

She looked up then.

He held his breath, unwilling to do anything that might stop her from the revelation she was about to let loose.

"I was…wondering if you'd…done any digging into Lou Rossi's business." She hesitated. "I mean…Troy did disappear on his way home from Lou's job site."

Her naive question spoke volumes to him. *A real babe in the woods.* He let his hand drop from her arm. He'd already considered the Rossi connection. But he'd hoped his suspicion would be proved false. "What do you mean?" he asked in mock innocence.

"I mean…could he have seen something—a drug deal…?"

She was being oblique. She might not, but police departments knew all about the special hassles construction companies faced in large urban settings. Their job sites were sitting ducks for vandalism, theft. He'd found no evidence of drug dealing at the Rossi site, but that didn't mean none had existed. Did she guess Rossi might have been the target of extortion?

Rand had already sketched this unpleasant possibility into his investigation. She needed to learn to suspect everyone until the case was solved—for her own good. After all, she was a lawyer. Why shouldn't he just toss his speculation out in the open?

A little practical life in the trenches would bring her closer to earth where the rest of them lived. And the shock might force her to blurt out something.

"You mean," he hardened his voice, "do I know if Rossi might have some connection to the Chicago mob?"

She gaped at him. Finally swallowing, she said, "I don't know what you're talking about."

He eyed her. Did *she* have any facts? He didn't want to think that Rossi paid protection—had, in fact, found no evidence of it thus far. Was this just supposition on her part? He had no facts and truly shattering her illusions about an old family friend wasn't his goal. Finding Nielsen was. "Then why did you ask the question?" Again, he bided his time.

"I…it's just…" Her cell phone rang and she answered it.

Rand looked past her, but listened to the few words she said. Something about the downtown fire station.

"I've got to go. Something's come up." Connie looked as though she was about to say more, but obviously thought better of it. "Thanks for the stroll." She offered him her hand.

He took her soft hand in his, but wondered what she'd do if he came closer and ran the back of his hand down her cheek. He let go of her. *I am definitely getting too personally involved in this case and with this woman. Connie, this is the last private conversation we will be having.*

She walked away quickly without looking back.

Despite all his sensible intentions, he admired the view of her, her head held high and her gentle sway as she walked away.

This fascination with Connie Oberlin had to

stop. *I've got to find out what happened to Troy Nielsen and get done with this case. I have no business taking pretty young lawyers out for afternoon strolls. Especially not Ms. Constance Oberlin.*

After leaving O'Neill, Connie marched down the street toward the main fire station. *Saved by the bell...well, cell phone.* "Maybe he'll forget what I said," she muttered to herself. "Why did I go to him?" She cringed. "He must think I'm some pathetic clinging vine—" She broke off her monologue.

Fire Station Number One loomed ahead of her. The doors were open. Rubber-booted firemen were washing already gleaming red fire engines. Some good-natured water-spraying elicited shouts and laughter.

Connie stood and watched, feeling the faint sprinkle of water on her face and then her ankles. The cheerful scene only made her feel more disheartened by contrast.

"Ms. Oberlin?" A strong voice hailed her over the melee.

She glimpsed a man in a fire chief's uniform, framed by an inner doorway and beckoning her. *Must be the man I'm looking for.*

To allow her to pass, the firemen pointed their hoses down, beaming at her. She walked past them to the fire chief and ignored the firemen's muted wolf whistles. She understood it was merely an extension of their high spirits. She was glad someone was enjoying this flawless summer day.

The fire chief accepted her hand and shook it firmly. "Let's go into my office."

Inside, he showed her to a seat on the other side of his vast desk and sat opposite her. "What can I do for you, Ms. Oberlin?"

"First, thank you for giving me some of your time. I'm—"

"No problem," he interrupted the gracious intro she'd prepared. "How can I help you?"

"I've studied the state fire marshal's report on the Depot Street fire. I was hoping you could help me understand better some of the notations he made." *And maybe some hope for evidence that would help my client.*

The fire chief nodded once. "I've studied that report myself. What do you need?"

Connie reached into her shoulder bag and pulled out her small leather planner. She flipped to the notes she'd made in anticipation of this interview. "First of all, the marshal mentions a *plant*. The context of the report led me to believe that in using this term he thought that the fire had been set."

"Correct."

She waited but he didn't elaborate.

"But when I went to the fire scene," she continued, "it was fairly obvious to me, as it was to the fire marshal, that the point of origin of the fire was the antiquated fuse box."

"Yes."

A man of few words. "But how could someone start a fire in a fuse box? I mean, apart from the old penny trick, which the fire marshal mentioned as unlikely."

The fire chief veered away from her comments unexpectedly. "I wonder how Sanders got fire insurance for that building."

"What?" She paused with her pen in hand.

"That building was scheduled to be torn down this year." The fire chief folded his hands on top of his desk and stared at her. "I heard Sanders didn't want to spend the money necessary to bring it up to code."

"But…" She fell silent as congealing cement settled in her midsection. *Sanders insured a building slated for demolition. And he thought he could get away with torching it?* That obviously was what this man was informing her of.

"Ms. Oberlin, as I said, I went over that report myself before you came. I know you're trying to find an out for your client." His voice became sympathetic. "But too much is against him."

"But—"

The fire chief held up his hand, silencing her.

She closed her mouth, realizing she didn't know what to say next.

"First, the smoke was black." The chief began ticking off points on his fingers. "That means a trailer, probably petroleum—"

"What's a trailer?" Connie scribbled this term into her planner.

"An accelerant. In this case, gasoline, which witnesses smelled at the scene."

"People? You mean firemen?"

"Firemen and a few passersby." He continued to the next finger, hammering another gaping hole through her case, through her. "The smoke was black. That tells us that gasoline was present.

"Second, the fire spread rapidly, more rapidly than a wood fire should have. By the way, a wood fire would have put out white smoke. Again, this points to an accelerant. Do you want me to go on?"

Acceding defeat, Connie shook her head and rose with all the dignity she could manage. "I won't take any more of your time."

"Ms. Oberlin, you probably touched on arson cases in your law school courses. But maybe you don't realize that very rarely does a district attorney choose to prosecute a suspected arson case."

"Why?" she asked the natural question. *Why didn't this surprise her?*

"Because often the D.A. finds it hard to prove arson *beyond a reasonable doubt* to a jury. So if the D.A. is bringing this to trial, he is sure of his grounds."

So numb she had trouble feeling her feet touch down, Connie nodded and walked to the door. He opened it and she left with only a murmured, "Thank you for your time." *For destroying my hope of finding something wrong with the fire marshal's report.*

The firemen had finished their washing and were busy shining chrome. *I have to come up with some possible suspects, someone else who might have profited from the fire or had a motive to set it.* Feeling hollow inside, Connie walked outside and lifted her face to the warm sun, closing her eyes. *I'd rather be anywhere, doing anything else today. Can't anything go right, Lord?*

"Hey, pretty lady!"

Connie opened her eyes and saw Chuck O'Neill jogging toward her. She groaned silently.

"How about a cup of coffee? The deli will be quiet now."

She took a step back from him. "No—"

"Come on," he coaxed. He hooked her elbow with his and tugged her to the curb. "You look like you need a cup of coffee and a few jokes."

"No." She couldn't argue with his take on her mood, but she had to return to the office. *Even if I don't want to get back before Grove and Maureen have left for the day.*

"Having a rough day?" Chuck murmured, letting go of her arm.

She nodded, arrested by his sympathetic tone.

"How about I walk you back to your office? Unless you're headed somewhere else?"

"No, I'm going..." She stopped. "How do you know where my office is?"

"I'm a detective, remember?" He claimed her arm again and they walked across the street together.

Connie allowed him to persuade her. If she let him walk her to the office, she wouldn't be left alone with her unruly thoughts—all of which seemed negative today.

"We're both the new kids on the block." Chuck let go of her arm when they stepped onto the opposite curb. "Are you getting a lot of razzing?"

"Not exactly." *No, I've just got stuck with an impossible case and a suspicious client and doubts about one of the senior partners. No big deal.* But there was something irresistible about Chuck's upbeat way. "What about you?"

"Shaving cream in my desk drawers and a tack in my chair aren't going to spook me." He chuckled. "We'll get through this."

"I'm glad you can be so optimistic." She wished all she had to deal with were childish pranks. The aching dead weight in the pit of her stomach hardened, clenched.

"We can't let it throw us. We've got what it takes."

She shook her head, grinning in spite of herself.

"Hey, someday this will all be behind us. That's

what my mom says all the time. Don't sweat the small stuff."

Troy must be found. But how? She had to defend Floyd Sanders. But how? Connie couldn't stop herself from asking, "What if it isn't small stuff?"

"Mom would tell you, in this life, most everything is small stuff. Mom has an eternal perspective."

Connie absorbed this. "I've heard of that, but sometimes it's hard to look that high or far."

"Then she'd remind you that God's eye is on the sparrow and all that stuff."

Connie closed her eyes for a moment, hearing the hymn play in her mind. *Thanks for the reminder, Lord.* "Your mom's right."

"Seen my brother lately?"

"Oh, I see him around," she said.

"Well, I was glad I saw you today because I wanted to see if you'd double with me and Sheila."

"Double?" She stopped and looked at him in astonishment.

"Yeah, you and Rand and me and Sheila go to a movie, grab a bite to eat."

"Your brother and I *aren't* a couple. He's the detective and I'm a friend of the victim. That's it."

"I know he's working on that case about your missing friend, but that doesn't mean you can't watch a movie together. You're not directly involved in the case. Not a witness or friend of a defendant. Your firm isn't involved at all."

"How do you know all of that?" She quickened her pace. *This is crazy.* Her office building sat ahead on the corner.

He shrugged. "I checked. My brother acts like I don't understand about conflict of interest, but I do."

She sped up. "I'm sorry, but—"

"Don't make a snap decision," Chuck continued, unabashed. "I want to impress Sheila on our first real date. My big brother the detective and the loveliest new lawyer in town."

Connie ignored his hyperbolic flattery. "Who's Sheila?"

"A very nice patrol officer. *Very nice,*" he reiterated with a smile. "Anyway, she finally said she'd go out with me but only with another couple. So what do you say?"

Connie shook her head, opened the door to her office building and tried to step inside.

Maureen stood in the doorway, obviously on her way out.

"Oh." Connie pulled up short. "I didn't see you there." *Were you standing there watching, waiting for me?*

Maureen gave her a friendly smile and walked out between Chuck and Connie.

"Hey, I'll give you a call tomorrow." Chuck tapped Connie's arm. "Think it over. We'd go out this weekend on Sunday night. Both Sheila and I will be off duty."

Barely listening to Chuck, Connie's face burned. Why had she let him escort her here? She recalled Maureen's advice about making friends with Rand. Would Maureen recognize Chuck as Rand O'Neill's brother? And what if she did? *I'm getting paranoid.*

"Hey?" Chuck waved a hand in front of her face.

"I don't think so." Connie hurried inside. When had all that she trusted, all that was normal, left her life?

He crept into the darkened church, lit only by flickering candles at the feet of saints. He rubbed his face with his hands, feeling the stubble on his chin and cheeks, smelling his own sweat, his sour breath.

He watched a priest come out of a door at the front of the sanctuary. He slid down silently and then under the old wooden pew. The marble floor underneath him was hard and cool. The priest's footsteps retreated and then the sound of a door shutting echoed through the cavernous space.

He wondered why he'd come. *I don't belong here of all places.* But it was cool and dark and empty. He let himself stretch out on the unyielding floor like some stray animal. *How did I get here? How do I get home again?*

Chapter Seven

"Hey, what'll it be?" the bartender asked with a welcoming grin.

"The usual," Rand said, testing to see if the man had finally put him down as a regular. To this end, Rand had been a steady but not flashy tipper. Tonight made two weeks since he'd started coming frequently to the sports bar of Troy's choice and nearing three weeks since the man disappeared. Had he won the barkeep's acceptance?

"Comin' right up." Soon, Rand's nonalcoholic brand slid in front of him.

With satisfaction, Rand nodded and ran his finger down the side of the cold, icy mug. He was in.

The place was still filling up for the night. On the big-screen TV, talking heads were discussing prospects for that night's baseball game. The barkeep wiped the bar in front of Rand.

Time for him to do what'd he'd endured all these nights to do. "I see a guy can place a bet here," Rand said low, holding his glass in front of his mouth.

The barkeep looked up, assessing. "Yeah, a sheet-maker for a bookie works the place. The boss doesn't like people betting over their heads though. We don't want no trouble."

"No problem. I just enjoy a bet now and then. Makes the game more exciting."

The barkeep nodded.

"Do I need an introduction?" Rand asked.

The man slapped the bar with his washcloth. "I'll tell him to give you a tumble when he comes in."

"Appreciate it." Rand turned his attention to the TV.

Again, he thought about Troy Nielsen. With all the places to go in Chicago, what kind of dad brought his little boys to a bar while his pretty little wife stayed home to study? And Rand's family wondered *why* he took a dim view of most people.

Connie's face came to mind. *If I told her that's what Troy had done, that was why the boys came here last week, she'd deny it. What is it with her and the canonization of Troy Nielsen?* He felt the familiar burn in his stomach that thinking of Connie and her hero worship of Nielsen always brought. That's why getting involved with someone in a case was stupid.

Over the blare of the TV and voices around him,

he replayed his mother's parting words to him last Sunday night—*I hear you had a pretty woman at your place Friday night?*

He'd perused her, but hadn't replied. Anything he'd have said would have given her something to comment on.

"That look won't work on me any more," she'd gone on. "It's time you got on with your life. Don't be mad at Chuck or Molly for trying to nudge you along."

Without commenting, he'd kissed her soft, lined cheek, thanked her for the meal and left her on the porch waving goodbye. He wished she'd just left things alone. Connie had come to his house only because of Troy Nielsen and for no other reason. He should thank heaven.

His stomach burned hotter. The pre-game jabber continued on the screen. He turned to it and made himself look deeply interested while he waited. Finally, the sheetmaker slithered inside and then around to his regular customers. He finally stopped to buy a drink at the bar.

Rand kept his eyes forward as though oblivious to the barkeep talking and nodding toward Rand. Within minutes, his prey dropped onto the bar stool beside him. "Hear you're looking for some action?"

Rand nodded. "Yeah, I'm Kennedy," Rand announced his alias as he shook the man's hand. "What's your point spread on the game tonight?"

The sheetmaker introduced himself as Bert and quoted the figures. "Make up your mind quick. I'm calling my bookie. The pitcher's on the mound."

"How about twenty on the Cubs to win?"

"Too low." Bert shook his head. "I can't take anything lower than fifty."

"That's a bit steep."

"Take it or leave it." Bert shrugged.

Rand considered. He doubted this was true, but maybe the guy was testing him. "Okay." Rand took out his billfold and handed Bert two twenties and a ten. "After last year's play-offs, I think the Cubs are going to bury the Marlins tonight."

Bert grinned. "Okay." The sheetmaker scribbled a number on a grubby pad of paper. "See you after the game." He headed to the wall phone by the entrance.

Rand returned to the game. He wondered what a string of fifty-dollar bets could have done to the Nielsen budget. Had Troy gotten in even deeper? Had he borrowed money to cover his bad debts from a loan shark?

That could explain his disappearance but Rand wondered again. Had Troy been trying to pay off gambling debts? Had the wife gotten any clue to where the money was going?

A commercial came on TV. The model advertising a new car wax had a face that reminded him of his sister Molly. He pictured her again as she'd burst in on Connie and him Friday night last week. She'd counted on his not objecting to the intrusion because there had been a stranger present. *Why can't they just leave me alone?*

He knew the answer already. When Cara had been murdered, he'd been forced down a harsh, black-as-Hades path his family didn't understand. They'd watched with concern from the sidelines, but had not walked it with him. No one could. It was a solitary trail one walked alone.

Would he find Troy Nielsen? Or would Nielsen's innocent little wife be forced to deal with betrayal, be thrust down a similarly soul-destroying path?

He sipped the cool liquid comfort, pushing stark memories away. He couldn't sit there and not drink. His excuse of having to drive home had covered his drinking nonalcoholic beer. *I'm here because this is my job. What about you, Nielsen?* Had Troy sat at this bar, drinking up and betting away cash his wife and kids needed? *What would you think if I told you that, Ms. Connie Oberlin?*

The game started at last and Rand watched it. The Cubs lost. But Rand was thankful it had wound up in only nine innings. He was grateful that this wouldn't come out of his pocket, but out of the department budget.

Bert came in and headed to Rand first. "Sorry, you should know the Cubs by now."

Rand gave him a rueful smile.

"No hard feelings?" Bert offered his hand.

Rand stood up. "No, you're not on the team."

Bert chuckled. "Nice doin' business with you. Place a bet with me anytime."

Rand nodded, threw his parting tip onto the bar and walked out. *Yes, everything's very friendly as long as I'm losing and paying up promptly. Did you have trouble doing that, Troy? How far over your head did you bet?*

,Late Tuesday afternoon, Connie walked down the courthouse steps, heading back to her office. She'd just sat in on an arraignment with one of the senior partners—Mulvaney, not Grove, to her relief.

Every time she glimpsed Grove in the office, her doubts about Uncle Lou circled her like starved wolves in a pack. She pushed her heavy foreboding away. Now her mind settled on a few affidavits she needed concerning the case.

But corralling her mind was becoming more of a problem. It drifted from the present to the past, to O'Neill. She pictured him walking with her in the formal garden behind the courthouse. Again, she heard him say, "You mean, do I know he might have some connection to the Chicago mob?" *He has to be wrong about Uncle Lou.*

"Ms. Oberlin?" A man stepped in front of her.

Connie stopped short. "Yes…yes?"

"I'm Ed Cudahy." He offered her a hand. "I live

a block from the warehouse that burned on Depot Street."

"Oh?" She shook his rough, wrinkled hand and waited. The thin man looked like a retired laborer, dressed in faded jeans and a frayed shirt.

"Mr. Sanders came around my neighborhood, asking if anybody witnessed the fire." His pale eyes shifted to the area around her, other people streaming in and out of the courthouse.

At his mention of Sanders, her nerves jumped to life with a jolt. "Yes?"

"I told Mr. Sanders I saw the whole thing. I have trouble sleeping, see?"

"Oh?" Connie paused while she yanked together her scattered thoughts. Then she asked the obvious question, "Do you think you have information that might help me in this case?" *This can't be happening. It's too good to be true.*

"I'll tell you what I seen and you can tell me if it helps or not. Okay?"

"Fair enough." Connie kept a tight rein on a sudden burst of hope. An eyewitness. "When can I speak to you?"

"Now would be good."

Connie glanced at her watch, afraid he might vanish when she looked up again. "I've got a few minutes to spare. Let's sit down on the bench over there." She pointed to a park bench under a large maple tree.

"Okay."

He loped along beside her and they both sat down on the shaded bench.

Summer breezes swirled around Connie's ankles. She opened her black leather briefcase and drew out a yellow legal pad. "I need your full name and address and phone number, please." She jotted down his answers. "Now, Mr. Cudahy, what did you see when you witnessed the Depot Street fire?"

"I couldn't sleep that night." Ed Cudahy fidgeted on the bench. "It was hotter than it shoulda been the beginning of May, you know what I mean?"

She nodded, not encouraged by the way his eyes kept avoiding hers. *Hear the man out.*

"So I was up making myself something to eat. Sometimes if I eat, I can go to sleep. Anyway, I rent the upstairs of an old house a block from the warehouse. I can see it from my kitchen window."

"The warehouse?"

"Yeah."

Connie's mood lifted a centimeter. She held herself in check. This might turn into something or it might not. *Go slow. Don't jump at this.* She nodded to the man.

"Well, I seen the sky that night light up in the direction of Depot Street. Like a flash. It made me curious and I went down to the alley to get a better look."

This didn't sound like evidence Sanders would want. A flash intimated arson. Who besides Sanders would have a motive for burning down the warehouse? "How far did you have to go to get a clearer view of the Sanders' property?"

"Not far. Some of the houses between the warehouse and where I live have been torn down. Urban development. Nobody wants to take time to keep up old property." He waved his hands with disgust. "Just tear things down."

Connie nodded and murmured sympathetically. *So far, so good.*

"Anyway, I seen somebody running away from the fire."

Connie sat forward, her pulse raced in spite of her caution. "Could you recognize him?"

"I didn't see his face." Cudahy sounded sure of himself. "But I could see, but the way he was runnin'—he's some young punk."

"How could you tell that?" She tilted her head, sizing up how he would look and sound on the witness stand.

"By the way he was dressed and the way he ran. An old guy couldn't run like that. The fire kind of streaked up in another flash and I saw him clear for a moment—a young punk like in a gang on TV."

"Not his face though?"

"No, too far away."

Connie mulled over the man's testimony. She'd have to do some serious checking before she'd use it. "Would you be willing to testify in court to what you saw?"

"Sure I would. Mr. Sanders told me that they think he set the fire himself to collect the insurance. But I know insurance companies." He jabbed a finger in the air as he continued. "They want your money but when it comes to paying out any, they'll grab at any straw to not have to."

"Thank you, Mr. Cudahy." Ideas, plans tumbled over each other in her mind. "I'll be getting in touch with you soon." She rose and shook his rough hand again. "I've got to get back to my office."

They parted and Connie walked the few blocks to her office. Had she just gotten a break in her case or would Cudahy prove to be a false lead?

On Friday evening, the third since Troy disappeared, Rand drove up the alley in Troy's truck behind the Nielsen house. Another chance to make contact with Annie and hope that something she'd say would provide Rand another possible lead.

With effort, he suppressed the guilty hope that he might be seeing Connie again. *I don't want to see her. I just want to see her reaction.* His conscience stung him for lying. *Okay. I shouldn't want to see her. I'll get past my fascination with her as soon as this case is over and done.*

Annie was waiting for him at the back gate. She looked as if she'd been crying and her hair wasn't combed. Was it just the continued stress of Troy's disappearance or something new? The twins stood on their tiptoes on either side of their mom. And Connie stood behind them, capturing his attention.

In contrast to Annie, Connie still wore her professional garb. She stood before him—fashionable, self-contained, alluring. Why didn't the inner and outer parts of her match? He could have cultivated a relationship with the cool, professional woman. But behind this facade was the passionate innocent who could believe no wrong of Troy.

"Daddy's truck!" The twins jumped up and down. "You brought back our daddy's truck!"

Rand climbed out and walked to the gate. Annie opened it for him. He handed her the replacement keys for the truck, keeping his focus on her, not Connie, though the effort taxed him. "I finally got it released this afternoon. Sorry, but they went over it with a fine-tooth comb for evidence, and that took time."

"Thanks." Annie could not have looked less grateful. Slow tears slipped down one cheek. "I'm sorry to cry, but for a few seconds when I saw the truck, it was like seeing Troy coming home…."

Connie squeezed her friend's shoulder. "Rand, have you, have you made any progress?"

No "hello." No "how are you?" Just the same question you ask me every time we meet. He brushed away his irritation. *What did you expect? A warm welcome?* "We still have no ransom note," he said, piling up point atop point against Nielsen. "We still have no paper trail to lead us to Troy. We still have no reports of anyone seeing him in Taperville or Chicago after the night he abandoned his pickup."

"I've been thinking—" Annie worried her lower lip "—about something." She looked down. "Boys, go in to Aunt Gracie and see if she needs you to set the table for supper." She turned her twins and pushed them toward the house. "Go on. Scoot."

The reluctant twins—still casting glances over their shoulders—finally trudged up the path to the house.

"What were you thinking?" Rand asked, his hands resting high on one of each of the round finials atop the gate posts.

Connie hovered beside Annie. Her eyes flashed a warning at him, which he ignored.

"Troy had been acting a little odd over the past few months," Annie confessed. She faced him, but stood to the side of the gate so their gazes didn't meet. She wove her fingers into the chain-link fence as though hanging on to what…reality, sanity?

Connie drew closer to Annie.

"What was he doing?" Rand prompted when Annie paused too long. Crosscurrents, sympathy for this brave lady and a zing of hope sliced through Rand. He tempered his eagerness. What she'd say might or might not help the case.

"We've always had our mail delivered to our door," Annie finally said. "Like everybody else I know."

"Yes." Rand agreed, wishing he could move her along at a faster pace. He rubbed his palms over the rounded finials.

Placing one hand just below his, Connie visibly braced herself also. His hand nearest hers tingled.

"But a few months ago, Troy went and rented a post office box in Taperville and had all our bills and business mail forwarded there." Annie rocked back and forth, making the fence links chink softly.

"What month was that?" He kept his tone even, knowing that anything might stop her from sharing these previously hidden facts. Annie Nielsen had lost weight over the past three weeks. Rand had seen this happen in so many other cases. *What's eating you, Annie? What else haven't you told me?*

She pressed her forehead into the chain links. "I think it must have been…near the end of March. He said it would be more convenient for him. I thought…I thought it was odd. But I was so busy studying for mid-terms when he brought it up that I didn't think anything much about it. He's always taken care of bills and did the banking. But now…" She glanced over her shoulder at Connie.

"Do you want me to go in, too?" Connie asked, taking a step back.

Rand waited to see what Annie would say. Would she want Connie to hear or was this too revealing for Connie's ears?

"No…no," Annie said, struggling with herself. "I told Patience when she called earlier. And you might as well hear it from me, too, Connie." She turned back to him. "Last night, it occurred to me it was nearing the end of July. That I needed to pay bills. I didn't even know if Troy had paid the June ones. But I didn't have any bills here to pay. And I don't have the key to the post office box."

Annie glanced up at him and then back down. "It disappeared with Troy. And I've never even been to that post office."

"Yes?" Rand thought he knew what was coming. *Poor woman.* But Connie's brow had wrinkled deeply. *You don't get it yet, do you?*

"So this morning I dug out some old bill receipts and called the utilities so they could tell me what I owed and I could ask them to switch our billing address back to the house." Annie's voice broke.

He realized he'd clenched his jaw. He loosened it, but clung to the finials, ready for what was to come.

Connie put an arm around Annie as though she sensed a stunning blow was about to fall.

"What did the utilities have to say?" Rand asked, now positive of what she was going to say. He shoved his hands into his pockets and leaned against the gate post, distancing himself.

"They all said the same thing. They said we are three months in arrears. *Three months.*" Still clutching the fence, making it chink, Annie looked at him, a wildness in her eyes. "Troy hasn't paid any bills in three months."

Connie gasped.

Rand glared down at the dandelions growing around the base of the fence.

Annie suppressed a sob. "And then…then I called the bank to find out what our balances were…. Our accounts have been closed. I don't have a dime." Annie began crying in earnest. "So you've been right all along." She clung to the fence, gasping between sobs. "Troy did plan this. He's been hoarding…our money, getting ready to leave us. The electric company said if it doesn't get at least partial payment soon, they'll turn off our… lights."

Connie turned Annie in her arms and hugged her. She looked to Rand over Annie's heaving shoulders. For once it wasn't an accusatory one. Disbelief and shock showed on Connie's face.

He stepped through the gate. So Nielsen, who'd been blessed with a nice wife and kids, had let them down. *And for what?* A sound of disgust summed up Rand's opinion of the man.

"How could he? He left us with nothing," Annie moaned. "How could he be so *cruel?*" Annie's pained voice cut through the silence hanging over Rand and Connie. He took no pleasure in the woman's horrible discovery. Or in finally watching Connie's illusions about Troy Nielsen shatter.

Rand wanted to tell Annie that the behavior she was describing might be that of a husband about to leave his wife, but it also described other possibilities. But he had no hard evidence to give her to back up the new trend of his suspicions. Better to say nothing than to say what might later be proved incorrect.

"Let's get her inside," he murmured to Connie. He shepherded Connie and Annie toward the house.

Hours later, Connie let Rand into her Volvo and they drove away from Annie's home. He'd planned to catch a taxi home, but had stayed at the Nielsen apartment hoping to pick up any possible lead or even a hint of one. None had come, but what he'd learned from Annie about the bills reinforced his own hunch.

"I still can't take it in." Connie stared through the windshield. "There has to be some explanation for why Troy would—"

"Would take all the money and run?" Rand couldn't keep the snide trace out of his voice.

Connie made no reply.

Rand's conscience nudged him. "Sorry. I'm not happy about what Annie found out today. It's just…I get so tired of this garbage myself. Annie's a sweet mother and the kids are great and…"

"And you obviously still think Troy has abandoned them?" Connie said, a warning in her tone.

Give it up. "And *you* think," Rand said acidly, "he's still a knight in shining armor and will return with the Holy Grail."

Silence.

"He can't have planned to leave Annie penniless.... There has to be some reason, some explanation—"

"Of what?" He made a sound of disgust at himself. Why did he want to make her see how nasty the world really was? Just because of what he'd suffered, did he need to mock someone who was struggling to deny the damning truth about a childhood friend? *He left them penniless, Connie, whether he planned it or not. He did it.*

"I don't know what has happened to Troy." Connie's knuckles whitened as she clenched her fingers around the steering wheel.

"Then we're in the same sinking boat. I don't know for certain, either." *Though I have a good guess.* Feeling even his bones were weary, Rand let the surliness drain from him before he went on speaking. "You know what I think and I know what you think. Let's just drop this, okay?"

"Okay."

Silence.

In it, his awareness of Connie expanded and sharpened. He watched her glance into her rearview mirror, slow to a stop, accelerate and rotate the wheel when they turned a corner. Then they were on the tollway out to Taperville.

The light from the dash and the tall sodium lamps gave a ghostly light to her clear, attractive features. Her distinctive scent, some expensive fragrance no doubt, was all around him. Her slender arm reached out and she snapped on the CD player. An eerie, Celtic melody filled the car. It suited the woman beside him, the woman who more and more was never very far from his thoughts.

For a moment, he let his imagination run wild and free. He imagined moving closer to the warm vibrant woman he sensed Connie Oberlin to be. He would touch her soft cheek and turn her face in his hands. *I would kiss your lips…*

He snapped off his imagination. His heart was jumping in his chest. *That's why I wanted to be the one to deliver the truck. I knew Connie would be there. I want to kiss her, hold her.* This admission left him reeling as if he'd just run into a wall in the dark. *No.*

On Monday evening, Rand's home phone rang. Suppressing a yawn, he picked it up.

"O'Neill, it's Connie." Her voice shook with emotion.

"What is it?" he asked, his pulse coming alive.

"Someone stole Troy's truck today."

Chapter Eight

Later that Monday evening at Annie's kitchen table, Connie perched, her hands frozen to each side of the seat of her chair. Then she broke her death grip and rubbed her eyes. They ached from reading fine print all day and from willing away unwelcome tears.

It seemed that the last month she'd scarcely been inside her own home, her new condo in Taperville. She'd spent years avoiding this apartment, coming only rarely to face Annie and Troy together. Now after his disappearance, she'd stayed every night, every weekend here with Annie and the rest of her family. *One crisis after another.*

O'Neill sat beside Connie, his brooding presence agitating her, attuning her to him. He'd insisted that he come and go over facts about the truck with Annie before she called the local police to report the burglary of the pickup. Connie was waiting to see what he would make of this. Would it bring them any closer to unraveling the mystery surrounding Troy's disappearance?

Annie had turned on only the light over the stove so that the kitchen was cast in shadows. Connie was grateful for the low light. It hid her despair. Rooms away, Jack and Grâcie were putting the twins to bed. Uncle Lou paced the kitchen looking like an angry bear. As if carved from granite, Annie sat across from Connie. She'd just explained why she hadn't noticed that the truck was missing until she'd come home after helping out at Jack's office just across the street.

"When are you going to find my nephew?" Lou barked at O'Neill, who had just opened his notebook and pen.

"I'm investigating every lead." O'Neill didn't look up from his pad. "But if someone doesn't want to be found, it makes it hard."

O'Neill's voice was devoid of inflection or emotion. It made Connie shiver, bringing gooseflesh on her arms.

"Troy can't have left his family." Lou slammed his hand down on the kitchen counter. "He's a good boy, my nephew."

The blow shuddered through Connie. Over the past week, her belief that Troy had been kidnapped had begun to splinter, revealing cracks. She ached over his betrayal of Annie. *Troy, there must have been a reason. Why would you empty out your joint accounts and leave Annie penniless and with no support?*

She had to find the extenuating circumstances so she could understand why Troy had behaved so out of character. *What am I missing, Lord? Why is this happening? What have I left undone that I should have done to help Annie, to find the truth?*

Her conscience stirred. Once before, she'd discussed with O'Neill the possibility that Uncle Lou might be involved in Troy's disappearance. What he'd told her in return had been too upsetting for her to deal with. His cynicism had sliced through her. *I can't be a coward any longer. I'm going to make O'Neill help me find out if Rossi Construction Company is involved with organized crime or not. And then if this had anything to do with whatever happened to Troy.*

"Rossi, how do you explain his letting bills pile up unpaid?" O'Neill asked, his pen in hand.

Connie focused on the way his long fingers gripped the pencil.

"What?" Lou halted.

"I was going to call you…" Annie rubbed the back of her neck and twisted her head as though loosening tight muscles. "But I couldn't bring myself to tell you."

"Tell me what?" Lou moved closer to Annie.

Annie looked to Connie, begging her silently to break the awful news to Uncle Lou.

"I'm sorry to have to tell you this." Connie's nerves tingled and she felt like crawling out of her own skin. She looked down at her hands and began tearing at a tag of skin beside her thumbnail. "Troy rented a post office box in Taperville and had all the bills forwarded there." The tag of skin ripped off, leaving a tiny red slit that stung.

Connie folded her hands together to stop herself from repeating this painful little act of frayed nerves. "Then he stopped paying bills in March." She couldn't put any emotion into her recital. Her voice sounded like O'Neill's. *This is not happening.* "Troy also stripped every penny out of their joint bank accounts. Annie is about to have her electricity cut off."

Lou exploded with Italian phrases, his usual way of venting anger.

Annie sat in stoic silence. Connie's hands knotted together under her chin. O'Neill leaned fractionally closer to her, but also waited out the eruption, merely tapping the blunt end of his pen on his notebook.

Uncle Lou's tirade finally subsided, and red-faced, breathing hard, he said, "You give me the bills. I'll pay them."

"No…" Annie made her voice stronger. "No, that's not right. You've helped us enough—bringing Troy's wages in cash to me every Friday. I can't let you shoulder Troy's responsibilities—*my* responsibilities—indefinitely."

Lou tried to interrupt, but Annie persevered. "I'm able to work. Jack said he can use me to do some clerical work at his office here in the neighborhood and Sandy said she'll watch the twins for me for free while I'm there. And I'll be getting a refund soon for the summer tuition I'd paid. I dropped everything before the cutoff date. You... I..." Annie fell silent.

"I'll still be paying you Troy's salary until we find him," Lou said stubbornly. He glared at O'Neill as if all this were his doing.

"We have to face..." Annie stammered. She reached up and took the older man's hand. "Troy may not...he may not..."

Connie's heart shriveled up as Annie tried to say the words: "He may not be coming back." *Annie, dear Annie. I loved you and your family long before I lost my heart to Troy. Troy, what did you do this for? What's the explanation? There has to be one. You can't have meant all this.*

O'Neill cleared his throat. "That was a pretty new truck. Was it paid for?"

Finally grateful for his persistence and ability to focus, Connie tried to shore up her defenses against her consciousness of him. She sensed Rand was choosing his words with exquisite care. Why did she doubt his sensitivity to Annie's pain?

Annie shook her head no. "I didn't think we needed a new truck, but Troy bought it at the end of

last December. He got a great price and a no-inter-
est loan on it because the dealer wanted to get it off
his lot before the new year."

"I wondered." O'Neill looked as though this had
told him something important—nodding to himself
and jotting another note down. "Who was the dealer?"

Connie eyed him. What had it revealed to him?

Annie named a large Chicago dealership.

"Let me call them. It might not have been stolen,
just repossessed. That's why I wanted you to wait before we called Hess." He pulled out his cell phone
and punched in a number.

Uncle Lou started to say something—maybe
"Troy wouldn't do that," but stopped himself.

"Would they break into a garage to repossess a vehicle?" Connie asked, pressing her hands together,
so she wouldn't start tearing at her own skin again.
"Is that legal?"

O'Neill shrugged. "Some of these professional
repossessing outfits aren't too picky how they get the
vehicles back."

Connie opened her mouth to ask another question.

He held up a hand, forestalling her. "Yeah, this is
Rand O'Neill," he spoke into the phone. "Taperville
police detective. I need to know if any of your men
picked up…"

Connie let O'Neill's low voice flow around her.
She watched the way his hand covered Annie's while
the other cradled the phone to his ear.

"Thanks." O'Neill hung up. "No, the pickup wasn't repossessed. But Troy only made two payments on it and it was on the repossession list for June. If it hadn't been in police custody after Troy's disappearance, it would have been picked up." He made eye contact with Connie.

She returned his gaze, her brow lifted, asking him why this was important.

"Troy had been notified of the repossession," O'Neill continued, not answering her unspoken question. "Annie, do you know where the truck's loan paperwork was filed? Here or a safety deposit box at a bank?"

Annie looked confused for a moment.

"Where did you and Troy keep your important papers?" Connie asked.

"It's in the file cabinet in the spare bedroom." Annie pointed to the small room opposite the bathroom. Connie rose.

Uncle Lou lumbered over and sat down in the chair Connie had vacated. His face was gray.

Connie felt like she should say something to the sorrowful man. But what? "Annie, is the cabinet locked?"

"No, there's a file folder in the top drawer." Annie covered the big hand Uncle Lou laid on her shoulder with hers.

Connie remembered having conversations like this as she had dealt with the details of her parents' funerals. But those painful conversations had ended when the departed had been interred. *This process goes on and on. For how long? If we don't find Troy, this could go on for years.* Tears began to well up from deep inside her.

O'Neill followed Connie. His coming with her nearly put her over the brink. She clamped down on an upsurge of weeping, kept it tightly concealed inside. She switched on the lights in the small room that had a desk, file cabinet and sofa bed where Connie slept most nights now. She slumped down on the sofa bed suddenly too tired to go on. "I can't believe this is happening," she whispered, choking down the tears.

Rand stood over her, wounded by the way she'd folded in on herself as if fractured by this latest blow. "I'm sorry," he whispered in turn.

As though drowning, she held up one hand to him.

He took it. "What do you want from me?" he murmured, not wanting Annie and Lou to hear them. "I can't change any of this."

"I can't face it." She stood and walked into his arms. "It's too much."

Knowing he shouldn't, knowing it was wrong, knowing he was taking advantage of her vulnerable state of mind, he folded his arms around her warmth and softness. He lowered his guard. *Just this once. Never again.*

He waited for her to pull away, to sever their connection. But she laid her cheek against his shoulder. When he felt her tears wet his shirt, he stroked her sleek hair and murmured consoling sounds. He forgot everything but the yielding form pressed against him.

Abruptly, she pulled away, turning from him. "Sorry. I shouldn't have done that. I don't know why I did." She folded her arms around herself as though chilled. "It's just so hard to see Annie going through this."

"I'm the one who should apologize." Rand's voice grated low in his throat. "I was out of line." To stop himself from reaching for her, he opened the top file drawer and began pawing through the files, looking at their labels. He pulled out one and began rifling through it.

"There must be a reason for Troy doing all this." Arms still around herself, Connie moved closer to him. "The bills, the accounts, now the truck…"

"Haven't you figured that out yet?" Rand looked at her over the folders, the file cabinet drawer between them.

"No, what explains it? What am I missing?"

He shook his head as he found the folder labeled Important Documents.

"Tell me," she pleaded an urgent whisper. *"Please."*

"No. I have no hard proof yet. When I do, I'll let you in on my reasoning."

"But why would Troy buy a new truck and then only make two payments?" She gripped the edge of the file cabinet. "It doesn't make sense."

"It does if he wanted an expendable asset for almost nothing." Forcing himself not to look at her, Rand inspected each of the papers in the file, birth certificates for both the boys, social security cards and finally, the loan agreement for the truck. It had been over twenty thousand dollars new. How much of that value had it retained over the past six months?

"What do you mean?" Connie gripped the file folder, their fingers touching. "If he owed money on it, it would be a liability not an asset and besides, the truck's been stolen."

"Yes, but maybe Troy stole it."

On Friday evening after work, Connie sat in her Volvo near Ed Cudahy's home. She'd driven around the neighborhood, starting at the burnt-out warehouse, then in widening circles and finally to Ed Cudahy's street. She got out and walked down the street.

The area had obviously gone to seed. Older homes had been cut up into apartments or rooming houses. Tall shade trees swayed overhead in the wind of a gathering summer storm. Connie felt the same unease churning inside her.

All week long, she'd battled with herself over walking into O'Neill's arms Monday night. *Why did I do it? Stupid, stupid, stupid. He must think I'm an...* Her mind couldn't come up with an appropriate label for her idiotic behavior.

And she couldn't accept that Troy would steal his own truck. Could Troy be that calculating, that selfish?

Her cell phone rang. She pulled it from her purse and paused on the broken and heaved sidewalk. "Connie here."

"Chuck here."

"Oh, hi, do you have that information for me?" She'd called Chuck to find out more about Ed Cudahy. She wanted to be very sure of her ground before she put any faith in his testimony.

"Sure. Nothing to it. Cudahy has a clean record. No arrests, no convictions. And," Chuck teased, "I promise his name will never pass my lips no matter how I'm tortured."

"Very funny. But thanks. It was quicker to have you check than to do it myself." *And much easier than calling your brother. Much easier.*

"No problem. Where are you?"

"I'm on his street. I wasn't able to get him by phone, but I wanted to see his backyard and how easy... Well, I don't have to go into that. Thanks again—"

"Don't hang up yet. Have you given the double-dating idea any more thought?"

"I'm sorry, Chuck." This had been the one hitch in calling Chuck O'Neill, but no matter what he said, she was not double-dating with the O'Neill brothers. A definite no. "I just don't think that would work out. But thanks, and remember if you ever need a favor from a lawyer—"

"I'll call you. Okay, but I haven't given up." He rang off.

Hanging up, Connie walked up the steps to Ed Cudahy's apartment, which was in an older two-story house. His hand-printed name was displayed on a strip of yellowed paper under wrinkled tape. She pushed the doorbell button under it and waited.

Finally, the door opened. A large-boned woman in a flowered housedress and apron looked out with a smile. "Who you want, honey?"

"I'm sorry. I thought I pushed Mr. Cudahy's button."

"Cudahy?" The woman stared at her and then twisted her face. "What would a pretty young lady like you want with that dried-up old coot?" The woman chuckled.

This forced Connie to grin. "He's helping me on a legal case—"

The woman gave her an astute look. "This about that warehouse burning over on Depot?"

"Yes, is he home?" Connie wondered if this woman might be another witness for her defendant.

"No. He's out. I answered the door because I saw you through the curtains. I own the house. I rent out the upstairs to him and another old coot. They're both out. Down at the neighborhood bar probably."

She nodded toward the end of the street, which was only three houses away. Neon beer signs advertised a corner tavern and liquor store there.

Connie was not too unhappy that Ed Cudahy wasn't at home. Maybe this woman would let her look around or maybe answer a few questions. "Did you see anything that night?"

The woman screwed up her face again. "Why don't we sit down on the porch?"

Connie allowed the woman, who limped slightly, to lead her slowly to a few sagging aluminum lawn chairs on the wide covered porch.

Her hostess eased herself into a worn plastic-webbed chair that creaked and rasped as she settled into it. "I love this porch. I try to spend most of the summer here watchin' my world walk by."

Connie remembered her manners. She offered the woman her hand. "I'm Connie Oberlin, a new lawyer in town."

"I'm Pansy Mayfield, an old lady in town." Pansy chuckled, wheezing slightly. "Call me Pansy, okay? Otherwise, when someone calls me Mrs. Mayfield, I feel even older."

Connie grinned again.

Pansy took control of the interview. "You're defending the warehouse owner, right?"

Impressed by the woman's perception, Connie nodded. "Yes, and Mr. Cudahy said that he saw the fire start from the window in his kitchen."

"Well, that's possible. They tore down the old Hagen house behind me last year. And they squashed that row of stores on the street behind Hagen's the year before that. I lived in this neighborhood all my life—child, wife and widow. It's bad to see how run-down it is. You'd think they'd furbish this part up with all the new construction going on here."

"That will probably happen." Connie had heard this before. "Property values will continue to rise and investors will come in—"

"Yes, and a bunch of yippies, yuppies—whatever you call 'em—will move in and want everything swanky." Pansy waved her hands toward her neighborhood. "I'll be ashamed to hang my bloomers out in the backyard on the line."

Connie chuckled again. Whatever Pansy lacked in "everything swanky," her wit made up for. "Did you see the fire that night?"

"No, but I sure woke up when the sirens came up the street." As if it had gone to sleep, Pansy tapped one foot on the wooden porch floor. "They were loud enough all right."

"Mr. Cudahy said that my defendant recently came through the neighborhood and spoke to people about the fire. The fire marshal thinks it was arson and my defendant says he's innocent."

"Your client named Sanders?"

Connie nodded. What had Pansy Mayfield's opinion of Floyd Sanders been?

"I didn't talk too much to him myself. But then I wasn't able to help him. I was like most everyone else."

"Like everyone else?" Connie asked.

"Asleep when the fire started."

Connie nodded glumly. "But Mr. Cudahy could have seen it out his kitchen window, right?"

"Yes, it's on the back. Why don't we walk around to the backyard so you can get a feel for what Cudahy might have seen?"

Connie had been about to ask permission to go to the backyard and see where Ed Cudahy's rear window was and the view of the warehouse. "Thank you. That would really help me."

"Sure." Pansy struggled to heft her weight out of the creaking lawn chair.

"I can go by myself—"

"No, no. It's good for me to keep this old body moving. When I can't get down the stairs, out into my yard, then I'll know it's time to sell the place and go into assisted-living."

Over the parched grass, Connie moved slowly, allowing the older woman to keep up with her. The wind swirled old newspapers and stray plastic grocery bags against the chain-link fence around the Mayfield house.

"Storm's coming," Pansy said. She walked over to the fence and pulled at the debris. "Looks terrible," she muttered to herself. "My husband, Lowell, would have a fit if he saw how this neighborhood has slipped."

Connie helped by picking up more debris ahead of Pansy. They made their way slowly along the fence to the backyard. Pansy wheezed beside Connie and then leaned against the venerable clothesline pole cemented into the ground in the middle of the backyard.

Pansy pointed out Ed Cudahy's back window and Connie looked around. And yes, it was possible that he could have seen a flash from his window. She walked through the back gate and the alley to see if Ed Cudahy could have seen someone running from the warehouse. And indeed he could have. Her spirits rising cautiously, Connie walked back to Pansy and escorted the woman back to her lawn chair.

"Did you get what you needed?" Pansy asked, out of breath.

"I did. The setting is the way he described it. Now I just have to find out who set the fire." Connie gave a mock shrug. "Do you have trouble with gangs in this area?"

"You mean like street gangs?"

Connie nodded.

"No, I don't think so, but maybe." Pansy's mouth twisted and she stared out into space.

Connie waited to see what the woman was thinking about, hoping it would be of help.

"Maybe this isn't important—" Pansy finally

spoke again "—maybe it means nothing at all. But the day after your client went through the neighborhood asking people what they'd seen the night of the fire, Cudahy had the back rent he owed me—in cash, all of it. In fact, he's paid up now through December. And that's odd because he just gets Social Security and a small pension. It may mean something or—"

"Hey, Beautiful!" Chuck hailed her as he pulled up to the curb and parked his red vintage convertible VW.

Connie turned and glared at him. *That's what I get for asking him for a favor.*

Chuck hopped out of the VW. "How about a bite to eat? I'm off for the weekend and Sheila's working again tonight."

Connie thanked Pansy, who was grinning knowingly at her, and stalked down the steps. "Chuck, I'm just about to drive into the city."

"To your friend's house?"

"Yes."

"You still gotta eat." He gave her one of his charming smiles. "You're not going to let me forage on my own, are you?"

From the end of the street, the silence exploded. Was it gunshots? Both Connie and Chuck swung toward the sound. A figure bolted from the corner tavern.

"They're robbing the liquor store again!" Pansy exclaimed from the porch.

Chapter Nine

Two more shots cracked. Chuck flew backward as if heaved by an unseen hand. He hit the broken sidewalk. Connie sprinted forward, her heart threatening to burst from her. "Chuck!" she screamed. "Chuck!"

He groaned.

Connie reached him and then looked up toward the shooter. She saw the robber's back disappear in the distance around another building.

"I need…get him." Chuck tried to rise.

"That doesn't matter now." She dropped down beside Chuck and pushed him back. A hole had burned through his white shirt near his shoulder and blood had flowed around it. More blood oozed up from the wound. Connie's head swam. Chuck lost consciousness.

"Is he hurt?" Pansy's shout penetrated the roaring buzz in Connie's head.

"Yes! Call 911!" With help on the way, Connie could concentrate. Her first-aid training flooded back, banishing the fuzziness that had swamped her. *Lord, help me do the right things. He wouldn't have been here if I hadn't called him.*

She shrugged out of her lightweight summer blazer and folded it into quarters, then pressed it down over the wound to staunch the bleeding. She closed her eyes, visualizing the wound. The blood had oozed, not gushed. *Thank you, Lord, it didn't hit an artery.*

People crowded around them. Connie ignored their questions—and prayed. Chuck's face whitened before her eyes. From behind, Pansy wheezed up, unsteady, pushing through the crowd. "They're on their way. They're coming."

Connie nodded, still breathing hard herself. When the blood seeped through the layers of cloth, she repositioned the blazer. So much blood. So much. *Come on, come on. Lord, where is that ambulance?*

Then the whine of a siren. A screech of brakes. Doors slamming. Two EMT's—one male, one female—shouldered their way through the crowd. They dropped down beside her. "Where's he hit?" the woman asked her.

"Near the shoulder, above the heart and lungs." Over Connie's head, thunder grumbled, giving voice to her agitation.

The male EMT pried Connie's bloody hands off

the red-soaked blazer and lifted it. Inspecting the wound, he spoke medical jargon to his partner. He applied a pressure bandage to the wound while the other started an IV.

Connie crawled backward, feeling the knees in her pantyhose rip and shred on the old sidewalk. She couldn't rise. She stayed on her knees, her head bowed, her hands flat on the rough concrete. The world swayed and expanded underneath her. Big fat raindrops plopped around her, sending up the smell of dust.

Two more EMT's appeared and strapped Chuck onto a rigid stretcher. They carried him away. The female EMT helped Connie up by the shoulder.

"I'm fine," Connie muttered, trying to stiffen her rubbery legs and arms. Cold raindrops pelted her back, her head. "How is he? Will he be all right?"

"I don't think it will be fatal." The woman turned Connie toward the street. "We're taking you with us."

"I'm all right." Connie shook her head. The world became a tilting carnival ride. Lightning crackled in the distance. She clung to the EMT's arm.

"You're in shock."

Connie couldn't argue with that. And besides, she wanted to go with Chuck, had to be with him, make sure he was okay. *Why did I tell him where I was? He wouldn't have been here if I hadn't opened my mouth. I should have known he wouldn't take no for an answer.*

* * *

Rain-drenched, Rand jogged through the E.R. entrance of the Taperville Hospital. He halted and gripped the cool edge of the reception counter. Wild panic was making his heart pound. Focusing, he snatched at the tail ends of his frayed composure.

This is why I wanted Chuck to go back to college. I knew something like this would happen. Pulling out his badge, he flashed it at the receptionist. "Taperville P.D. One of our men—my brother, Chuck O'Neill. Shot. How is he?"

She ran her finger down a list in front of her. "He only arrived minutes ago. He's been taken to X-ray. Please take a seat—"

"Rand," Connie called him from a chair along the wall in the sparsely populated waiting area.

"Connie?" He turned and hurried to her. "What are you doing…what happened to you?" Dried blood spotted and smeared one of her fashionable suits. The knees of her stockings were ripped out. She'd obviously rubbed her face with her hands and left trails of blood and grime there. She looked totally out of character and utterly defeated. He stifled the urge to gather her into his arms. "You're a mess."

Big tears gathered at the corners of her eyes and trailed down her grimy cheeks. He sat down beside her and clasped her sticky hands in his. *This can't have anything to do with Chuck. They couldn't have been together. No.* "Were you in an accident?"

"No, no…" She swallowed sobs. "Your brother. Your brother…shot."

Rand swore and pulled her close. "Tell me you weren't with Chuck when he was shot. *Tell me.*"

She rubbed her face against his chest. "I saw it happen. It's all my fault…." Tears overwhelmed her voice.

He pressed his face into her mussed hair, smelling faint perspiration born of fear. "No."

This was worse than he thought. His brother shot. This woman… *I wanted her to see life as it is, but not like this. And what does she mean it was her fault? What have you been up to, Connie?*

"*Rand!*" his mother's voice hailed him from the entrance and he looked up. "Where's Chuck?" His mother was pale and gripping his father's hand. "They called us. They say he's been shot."

Rand stood, pulling Connie up with him. His arm hooked under hers, keeping her close. He faced his mother and father. "I haven't seen him yet. He's in X-ray."

"What happened?" His mother rushed toward him and grasped the hand he held out to her. His father hovered behind her.

Connie pulled away from Rand. "It's all my fault. He drove up to talk to me. We were…talking on the sidewalk and—"

Rand took her elbow in his. "Whatever happened—it's not your fault."

Connie looked at him and then continued in a tight-squeezed voice. "A man robbed the liquor store. It was on the corner just a few houses away. Chuck shouted for him to stop." She covered her quivering mouth with her hands. "He turned and shot at Chuck." Tears spilled from Connie's brown eyes.

"Rand's right." His mother patted her arm. "You couldn't have known someone was going to rob the liquor store."

Connie shuddered and wiped her mascara-smudged cheeks with her fingertips. "I—"

"Are you the O'Neill family?" the receptionist called to them. "The doctor will see you now. This volunteer will take you to him."

Rand's pulse jerked and sped at an even faster tempo. He wanted to say something comforting to his parents, to Connie. Words failed him. Deep inside, he yelled incoherently at God. Anger, rage, outrage.

Connie moved to sit back down, but Rand pulled her along with them. She gave him a startled glance and then hurried to keep up with him.

In silence, Connie stood side-by-side with Rand at her condo's front door. Back at the hospital, though Rand had offered his services, his mother had insisted that she and their dad would stay the night with Chuck.

Before Connie and Rand left, Chuck had regained

consciousness. He would be released in twenty-four hours. No complications were anticipated. The bullet had gone clean through, hitting nothing vital. Connie could breathe again.

"Thanks for the ride home," Connie murmured, unlocking her door. "I'll get a neighbor to drive me to my car tomorrow."

"No problem." Rand gave her his shuttered look.

"I wish…I wish…" She couldn't finish her sentence, *I wish this hadn't happened.* That was understood. She looked up into Rand's face, so near hers. What she read there arrested her.

Unlike Chuck's, Rand's face never looked cheerful. But now the lines of his face had deepened into pitched gloom. Connie recalled the other time he'd looked like this—that evening in his kitchen when he'd blurted out his wife had been murdered.

I can't let him go home alone like this. "Come in." She pulled at his arm. "Come in."

"No." He turned to go.

"Yes." She gripped his sleeve and tugged him toward her.

"I'm going to the station and see if they've apprehended the suspect."

"You can call them." She cast around for a reason for him to stay. "I don't want to be alone." *That's the truth. And I don't want you spending a sleepless night at the department or home alone until…* She gave his sleeve another pull, refusing to release him.

Unexpectedly, he permitted her to draw him inside and lock the door behind them. "For a bit," he mumbled.

She'd persuaded him to stay. Now what was she to do with him? Connie led him through the foyer to the living room which opened onto her deck. "Why don't you call in and get the information you want? I have to go get out of these clothes."

Her blouse and skirt, spotted and stained with a murky brownish-maroon, had stiffened where the blood had spattered and smeared. The sticky-starchy sensation rubbed against her, stirring her mind to flashes of Chuck's body jerking with the impact of the bullet, the sound of his gun clattering to the sidewalk, her throat raw from screaming... She shoved these sensations away. "I'll...I'll be right out."

She escaped up the steps to her ivory and mauve bedroom and bath suite. The door had hardly shut behind her and she began stripping off the foul clothing. She rolled all of it, even her underthings, into a ball and shoved them into a corner of the room. These rags would all go into a trash bag tomorrow. She headed into the shower and twisted on the faucet.

Stepping under the warm spray, she let the water sluice away the awful memory of Chuck's blood and its traces on her skin. She glanced down and saw its stain flowing away, down the drain. She closed her eyes, willing away stark images that had flooded back.

Within minutes, she walked down the steps wearing a pair of blue shorts and a white shirt. Her still-wet hair hung over one shoulder, occasionally dripping onto the light berber carpet under her bare feet. She drew in a deep sigh. "I'm starved…." She halted. Rand had disappeared. She took in air again, steadying her jumping nerves. "Rand?"

"Out here." His voice came from the deck.

Reassurance swamped her. He hadn't left. She hurried down the rest of the steps and out to join him. Under her bare feet, the deck boards were still damp from the recent rain.

He stood alone, his stiff back to her. In that moment, she saw that this was the essence of Rand O'Neill—a man alone in the world with his back to all. If Troy had truly betrayed Annie or turned up dead, would this being separated, feeling distance from others be her reaction, her future?

To be rid of this presentiment, she shook herself, fanning her wet hair around her shoulders, flinging droplets that fell and clung to her face and bare arms. "I don't have a beautiful view like you do," she softened her voice, coming up behind him.

He turned to her. "They haven't caught him—" his voice was devoid of life "—but they've finished interviewing all the witnesses."

"He was wearing a ski mask." Connie offered this pitiful fact, shrinking from the way Rand was looking at her.

"Yes, but he had a distinctive voice." Rand's gaze

was glazed, glacial. "The liquor store owner thinks he knows who it is."

"Good." She tucked her cold hands under her arms. "I hope they find him and quick."

"I'm sorry you had to go through this." Rand sent his words at her, shards of ice.

"I'm more sorry for Chuck." Connie stared at her bare toes that had curled up, chilled by Rand's stark voice.

"Chuck knew what he was doing when he became a cop. I warned him enough times."

The frigid cynicism of Rand's tone looped a tight cinch around her heart. This man had a reason to feel the way he did. When his wife was murdered, he'd suffered a terrible loss. One he obviously hadn't put behind him. *This is none of my business.* But thinking that was easy. Acting on it was hard.

Make that impossible. Connie dropped her arms. "Come inside. Neither of us ate. I'll throw together one of those bags of frozen stir-fry."

"No, I—"

"Let's just eat a bite and then you can go home and I'll go to bed." Somehow she couldn't let him go without giving him something, even if it was only frozen stir-fry. "I'm not the domestic type, but I can follow the directions. Come on." She touched the sleeve of his wrinkled shirt and glanced up.

In the glow from her neighbor's patio light, his eyes still glinted dangerously, ominously bleak.

She leaned closer to him for only a moment. "Don't leave me alone yet," she whispered and then released his sleeve.

His unnerving gaze flickered over her and he moved forward. She led him back into her living room. He followed her, but unwillingly.

"Make yourself comfortable," she recited the polite phrase. To put him at ease or herself? She made herself be honest. His being here ignited a physical tension she knew he must be aware of also. Why this was, she refused to probe. She needed to defuse this intensity that crackled between them. Then she could send him home in good conscience.

He rolled up the sleeves of his white shirt and then heaved himself onto one of the stools at the kitchen bar. Ignoring the way her mind tracked his every move, she busied herself with the frying pan and oil. Soon the fragrances of oil and soy sauce filled the room.

"Aren't you going to ask me anything about Troy?" he goaded her, mocking her.

Connie detected an urgent undercurrent in Rand's tone. What was it? It sounded like it was prompted by more than the emotional distress caused by Chuck's being wounded.

"Well?" he said, needling her.

Switching the burner lower, she turned to him. "What do you want me to ask you?"

He switched topics again. "Do you think a meal will send me home happy?"

She eyed him, again sorting through his motives. *What do you want from me, Rand?* "The doctor said Chuck will be all right."

"He could be dead."

"So could I." The terror she felt when Chuck had been shot jarred her again. She shivered, but lifted her chin. She wouldn't let Rand take his emotional backlash out on her.

"Yes, you could be." His voice was harsh. "Both you and my brother could be lying cold on slabs in the morgue now."

"Your point being?" she asked sharply.

"Have you finally begun to see reality?" He hunched forward, his elbows on the counter. "Your old friend Troy may eventually turn up. But when he does, he isn't going to come out squeaky-clean, perfect like you think he is. He wasn't kidnapped."

She took the hot pan off the burner and faced him. Then she voiced her question aloud. "What brought this on?"

"People don't think," he said without looking at her. "They go through life with blindfolds on. They don't even realize they've been walking on the edge of a cliff until it's too late. Your friend Annie ignored big flashing neon signs that should have alerted her that something was very wrong with her marriage."

The unseen connection between Rand and her had become a battle front. Waves of anger emanated from him, surging against her, fast and hot. "What signs?" she demanded, trying to make him deal in facts, not fury.

He ignored her. "He buys an expensive truck they don't need. Gets a post office box in another town. Diverts all their mail to it. Abandons the truck he's only made two payments on *right* when it's about to be repossessed. When the truck is released from the impound, it disappears."

"What is your point?" Connie moved toward him.

"You still don't get it, do you?" He stood up, shoving back the stool.

"I get that you're upset because your brother was shot today. I get that."

"You're so naive you can't even believe that good old Uncle Lou might be hand in glove with the mob—"

"What's your point?" She flattened her palms on the counter between them.

"Troy was up to his eyeballs in debt." Rand flung these words in her face.

She refused to be intimidated. Talk was cheap. She clenched her jaw and demanded, "How?"

"Gambling. Your good old buddy Troy—Mr. Perfect-husband-and-father—was betting way over his head."

Connie gawked at him.

He returned her regard. He kept his hands folded in front of his face as he spoke. Was he saying this just to mock her?

"Explain this to me." Connie gripped the edge of the counter to keep herself from lunging at him.

"Your…friend…Troy—" he paused to emphasize each word as if she didn't understand much English "—needed cash to pay gambling debts—*if* I'm not mistaken. And I rarely am. He showed all the signs of a gambling addiction out of control."

"But—"

"Let me explain to you the finer points of the dangers of gambling," he said in an annoyingly patronizing tone. "Loan sharks give two types of loans. The first is the 'knockdown' where weekly payments include principal and interest. It's like borrowing two thousand dollars and making fourteen payments of two hundred each. In the end, the poor borrower pays back twenty-eight hundred dollars."

Connie glared at him.

"The second type of loan is the 'vig.' That's a six-for-five loan where a loan of five dollars on a Friday incurs a payment of six dollars the next Friday."

Connie made a dismissive sound.

Rand ignored her and went on. "But the worst of loan sharks, besides their resorting to violence, is that if unpaid, the loan is not considered paid until *both* the interest *and* principal were repaid together. In this way, the poor borrower will pay off the original amount many times before the debt would be considered paid. That's the hole I think Troy Nielsen dug himself into."

Fuming, Connie tried not to snap at him. "That's *your* explanation then?" she asked in a stiff tone.

"Yes, that's *my* explanation of the facts surrounding Troy Nielsen's *abandoning* his family."

She turned her back to him. *He's baiting me. I won't give in and give tit for tat.* She put the pan back on the burner and whisked the vegetables and chunks of chicken around inside the pan. They sizzled and gave her a reason to face away from him.

"So you won't take my bait?" he taunted.

"You're upset—"

He muttered something under his breath. "I sure am. Didn't today teach you anything? This is a nasty world, where punks rob liquor stores and shoot anybody who tries to stop them. A world where men gamble money away and ditch their cute little wives and children."

She refused to answer him. The vegetables and chicken hissing in the sauce, she slipped the frying pan off the burner again. Rand said no more and she sifted his words over and over in her mind, trying to get to what they really signified. From a cabinet, she lifted down two plates and divided the stir-fry mixture between them. From a drawer, she pulled out cloth napkins and tableware.

Turning, she placed the plates on the bar—one in front of Rand and one on the place beside him. She reached in the fridge and took out a pitcher of iced tea. She poured two glasses and then sat down beside him—all without looking into his eyes.

"Don't have any answers for me?" Rand's voice sounded jagged, unsettled.

"I hear a lot of wild and unpleasant speculation, but no proof." She held her fork over her plate, her reluctant appetite bailing on her. "Do you know for certain that Troy was gambling?"

"No, but—"

"Do you know for certain that Uncle Lou has ties to organized crime, not just suspicion?" She forestalled him with an upraised hand. "But real proof?"

"No, but—"

"When you have proof that Troy did more than bet on an occasional football game or proof that Uncle Lou has a connection to the mob, then I'll believe it." Connie laid her fork down and rubbed her tight forehead. *This has been a dreadful day, Lord.* "Now eat your stir-fry before it gets cold."

He made a sound of disgust. "You are one stubborn person."

"It takes one to know one." A hint of dark humor crept into her tone.

"Don't try to get around me," Rand warned.

"I never try to do the impossible." She closed her eyes. "Eat your food. We're both tired."

"Meaning?"

"Meaning, we're both tired." She opened her eyes and dragged in air. "And hungry." She followed her own advice and forked in a mouthful of food. Her stomach seemed to sigh with relief.

He finally picked up his fork and began eating.

She finished her first mouthful and sipped her iced tea. The time had come to face her fears. "I think you're right though. I think we should check out Uncle Lou and see if anything was going on at that job site that might have put Troy in danger. He might have seen something he wasn't supposed to."

"How do you fit," Rand asked her, still obviously resisting her effort to soothe him, "all the other evidence we've uncovered about Troy with Lou's job site?"

"Everything will fit *when* we've found out the connection. Not before."

He humphed. "Maybe in your life everything fits together neatly, but not in the life I know."

Chapter Ten

The next Monday morning, Connie sat behind her desk. Floyd Sanders once more sat across from her. She'd followed up on every point that Ed Cudahy had suggested. She'd contacted the police about possible gang activity in the warehouse area and asked about any previous acts of arson or serious vandalism there also. Nothing had popped up as promising.

One question nagged at her that she had to ask Floyd Sanders. Or did she? Her stomach churned. *Do I really want to know the truth?*

"Yes, indeed." Her client rubbed his hands together. "Things are coming together. The D.A. isn't going to be happy when he hears Cudahy testify, is he?"

Connie stared at her client. She just wanted to lay her head down on the desk and weep. The district attorney would indeed be unhappy to hear Ed Cudahy's testimony. But in the long run, she might be even un-happier if anyone found out that Floyd Sanders had indeed paid for the man's testimony.

Mr. Sanders, did you pay Mr. Cudahy…to prompt his memory? That was a version of the question that hovered in her mind, making her miserable. *I didn't know I could be such a moral coward. Why didn't I ever* seriously *contemplate that I might be asked to defend someone I think is guilty?* The glib discussions in law school about this hadn't gone deep enough, hadn't portrayed how awful this actually felt.

"I told you that fire marshal didn't know what he was talking about. *Arson.*" Floyd Sanders made a sound like a tomcat spitting. "I'll give him arson. If it was arson, I didn't do it. And I'll be happy to take the stand and tell the D.A. so."

Did you pay the teen Ed Cudahy described running away to start the fire? Or was that just the most believable explanation you could come up with?

Her client didn't seem to notice her silence. He rubbed his hands together again. "Well, if that's all, I'll be off. Having lunch with a friend of yours."

Connie looked up. "What?"

"Lou Rossi." Floyd Sanders actually straightened his lapels. "Wants to use me as a supplier for lumber for that new subdivision he's bankrolling out west of town."

Stunned by this news, Connie rose—with effort—

and offered Floyd Sanders her hand. "I'm happy to hear you're doing so well in spite of your losses."

After their handshake, he pointed his index finger like a pistol at her and smiled. "You get me off this arson charge and everything will fall into place. I'll come up smelling like a rose."

Connie tried to smile.

He leaned forward and claimed her hand again.

Involuntarily, she drew back.

"There will be a little bonus for you when you get me off. Don't worry," he lowered his voice, "your partners don't need to know anything about that."

He left whistling.

As if on cue, Maureen walked by Connie's office and waved at her through the glass. *She can't be watching me. She's just going about her business as usual. I'm being ridiculous.*

Connie sank into her chair, folded her arms on her desk and laid her head on them. "This is just too much. God," she muttered, "why is all this happening? Troy disappearing, Chuck getting shot, my getting stuck with the worst first client in history— why?"

She propped one elbow on the desk and hoisted her chin up onto her hand. *I have to get out of here. Now.*

She leaped up, clutched her shoulder bag and zipped out the door. She was down in the lobby before she gave any thought to her destination. Walking to her car in the nearby parkade, she decided she knew where she wished to go.

Within minutes, she was striding down the hospital corridor to Chuck's room in the hospital. She slowed, wondering what she'd say to him, why this was the place she wanted to be now.

Rand's pretty, young-looking mother shot out of Chuck's room and nearly collided with Connie. "Oh, hi!"

Connie smiled with effort. Why hadn't she guessed Chuck's mother might still be here? "Hello, Mrs. O'Neill—"

"Call me Dorcas, dear. After all you did for our Chuck yesterday, you're very dear to us."

"But I didn't do anything—"

"The doctor told us that Chuck wouldn't be getting out so soon if you hadn't known how to administer first aid." Giving an affectionate smile, she squeezed Connie's arm.

Connie blushed with embarrassment.

"Anyway I'm glad you're here. My husband went to work this morning as usual. So I'm here alone with Chuck. And now, Molly was just admitted downstairs!" Dorcas danced on her toes with excitement. "She went into labor early and I have to take her little girl home with me. And now Chuck needs a ride to his place and I can't be in two places at once. I tried to call Rand, but he's not in his office."

Connie's head reeled with all this information.

"Fine. You go ahead. I'll take care of getting Chuck home."

"Thanks." Dorcas hugged her and then laughed. "Everything happens all at once." She hurried off toward the elevators.

Connie felt like calling after her, "You said it." Instead, she walked into Chuck's room.

"Hey, beautiful lawyer!" Chuck greeted her.

"Doesn't anything dampen your spirits?" she asked wryly, moving over to his bedside.

"Well, I could be dead today. That puts everything into perspective, doesn't it?"

She sank into the bedside chair. "I had a nightmare last night that you had."

With his good arm, he reached toward her. "Hey, I'm fine. Molly's having her baby and Larry's going to be happy about that. He told me last Sunday that he didn't know if he would last if Molly went past her due date."

"*He* wouldn't make it?" Connie exclaimed.

"Yes, you've only met Molly once. Believe me, she's got what it takes to make a strong man shake in his shoes."

In spite of herself, Connie laughed out loud. "How can you make me laugh when yesterday I saw you shot? What does it take to get to you?"

Chuck sobered before her very eyes. "Mom and I were talking about you late last night."

Connie sat up straighter. "Me?"

"Yeah, you probably can't see it because you haven't known him for very long, but you're having an effect on Rand."

"Me?" she repeated.

Chuck nodded with a solemn set to his lips. "He isn't quite as distant, quite as grim."

Connie shook her head. "You're right I didn't know him before, but he's still distant." *And grim and…wounded.*

"Just don't give up on him, okay? You're good for him."

Connie wouldn't answer Chuck directly. "I hear you need a ride home. I have wheels."

"As soon as—" Chuck broke off. "Oh, here he comes."

A young doctor breezed in, clipboard in hand. "No complications. Everything looks good. A nurse will visit you at home daily for the next week to change your dressings. Any questions?"

"Are you sure he's ready to go home?" Rand's gruff voice came from the doorway.

Recognition shivered through Connie. She looked past the doctor and glimpsed Rand framed by the door. His face was cast into shadow. But then that was always the case. His face, his eyes, always appeared in eclipse.

"Yes, your brother is a healthy, strong young man. He'll be off work for a week and then desk duty for another. Then he should be fine."

Rand nodded like a stern schoolteacher.

The doctor chatted another few moments about two prescriptions he was writing that Chuck needed to have filled, and then the physician trotted out the door to the next patient.

"What are you doing here, Connie?" Rand asked, walking toward her.

In spite of his rude question, Connie's unruly pulse sped up at Rand's approach. The desire to take his hand nearly overwhelmed her.

"That's what's so wonderful about my brother," Chuck chimed in. "He's always ready to give a cheery welcome to all."

Rand merely gave his brother a dark glance.

"I wanted to see how he was." Connie gave the safe alibi, forcing herself to breathe normally. In a show of strength, she lifted her chin, silently telling Rand not to try to intimidate her.

"She's going to drive me home," Chuck informed Rand.

"I came to do that," Rand said. "And I brought you clean clothes from your apartment." He handed Chuck a white plastic grocery bag.

"She's cuter. I'll ride home with her." Chuck accepted the bag and in turn, handed Rand the prescription scripts the doctor had left. "You can stop and get these filled and then meet us at my apartment."

Rand grasped the slips of paper. He gave Connie an unreadable glance and then relented. "Okay." He turned to leave.

Again, Connie nearly reached for him. Didn't he realize how his actions revealed his need for comfort, for…some affection?

"My brother, always a charmer," Chuck said, grinning.

Connie tried to smile for Chuck's sake. Rand was acting as if she were responsible for Chuck's wound, which only yesterday he'd objected to. Had he assumed for himself that guilt today?

Not very logical. But it seemed that Rand had an irrational desire to assume responsibility for everything. And realizing this—more than anything—had begun releasing her from any feeling of guilt. She rose. "Chuck, I'll step outside and let you get changed." She retreated into the hall, closing the wide door behind her.

Rand stood in the hall. "I'm sorry if I sounded rude." He managed not to sound sorry at all. "I just didn't expect to see you here this morning."

Me, neither. Connie managed a half smile, though her mouth was parched. "I had to see that he was all right. I couldn't stay away." *I couldn't stand another moment at my office.*

Coming down the hall, a pretty redhead hailed Rand. "Hi, is that Chuck's room?"

"Hi, Sheila," Rand said. "Yes, he's just getting dressed to leave."

"Oh." The young woman looked disconcerted. "I didn't know he'd be getting out this soon—"

"Sheila!" Chuck opened the door a crack and beamed at her. "Come in. I need help getting into this shirt."

The redhead walked past Connie but with slow, reluctant steps. "Are they sure you are well enough to go home?"

"I have two eyewitnesses." Chuck nodded toward Connie and Rand. "Doc says I'm good to go."

"Well, okay." The redhead blushed, taking a step back. "Guess you don't need me."

"I sure do. Come in and help me with this shirt." Chuck winked at Connie. "And then you can drive me home. Rand and Connie were just leaving to go pick up my prescriptions." Chuck gave them each a telling look. "They'll drop them off at my place."

Rand appeared stolid, watchful. Sheila still looked hesitant.

Connie forced a smile. "Yes, please take Mr. Cheerful off our hands. He's just about to gag us with all his…his *jollity.* Maybe you can convince him that getting shot isn't a picnic." Since Rand looked frozen to the gray linoleum, Connie took his rock-solid arm and piloted them both away. "See you later, Chuck."

Though she sensed resistance, Rand allowed her to lead him to the elevators. They got in and Connie pressed the ground-floor button. The doors closed. She and Rand did not look at each other. What should she say, do? Offer to leave and let him deliver the pills?

"You can come with me to the pharmacy," Rand conceded, surprising her.

"I—I…fine." She didn't want to be with him. She didn't want to be parted from him.

Outside the hospital, the day was heating up. White gulls from distant Lake Michigan screeched over the parking lot. Unbroken blue, unmarred by clouds, stretched edge to edge on the canvas of the sky. In silence, they walked from the hospital to Rand's car. The heat of the day settled over them, suffocating.

He opened the door for her and handed her the seat belt. His behavior was formal, overly polite—an attempt to keep his distance from her? Did he feel the thread that connected them becoming taut? He got in on the other side and off they went.

"I'm playing hooky," she confessed to his profile. "After last night, I just can't concentrate." *I don't want to think about Floyd Sanders or Chuck getting shot or Uncle Lou—or you.*

"I'm a little out of it myself," Rand admitted.

She let this pass without comment. "Did anyone tell you that your sister is in labor?" she asked, trying to keep the conversation away from emotional potholes.

"No."

"Your mother went down to get their little girl and take her home so Larry could stay with Molly."

"I see," he said.

What a conversation. "That redhead was Sheila? The one Chuck wants us to double-date with?"

"Yeah. So he asked you, did he? What did you say?"

As usual, the man beside her gave nothing away. What had he thought about the concept of their double-dating? "Probably the same thing you said." Connie watched him from the corner of her eye. "We're not a couple. We're just involved in a case."

"That's what I said," he agreed. Mt. Rushmore showed more emotion than the man beside her.

Rand drove to a drive-in pharmacy's window. He switched on an easy-listening station on the radio to fill up the tense silence that yawned between them.

Connie turned the Sanders case and Lou Rossi over and over in her mind. A prompting, an urging to bring these topics up with Rand, gnawed at her. Of everyone involved, Rand O'Neill wouldn't pull any punches. She'd get his version of the truth. And unfortunately, it would be bitter but probably factual.

Weighing the differences between Rand and herself, she looked out the window as they drove to Chuck's apartment. Why did Rand make her feel so inexperienced? So green?

Mike Petrov, Annie and Gracie's dad, was older and wiser than she, but he never took the dark view of things. He always had hope. But then Mike loved God and believed in providence. How many times had she heard Mike recite Romans 8:28, "'In all things

God works for good with those who love him whom he has called according to his purpose.'"

"Want to go in?" Rand asked.

"No, we'd just be in the way." *And I must make a decision. Can I discuss my worries, reveal my weakness to you again? Could we actually confront Lou? Do I trust you or not?*

"Okay, I'll drop it off," Rand replied, "and then come down and take you back to your car."

She nodded absently. She found herself tearing at the skin on her thumb again and knotted her hands together to stop herself.

He left her parked at the curb, the motor and air conditioner running. She chewed her lower lip and fretted. *There's only one way to find out what I want to know and only one person who can help me. But do I want to face all this after what happened yesterday?*

She recalled watching Chuck take the bullet and then the churning of her stomach when Annie had revealed Troy's behavior starting in March.

Within minutes, Rand returned. "Okay—"

Connie looked at him and made her decision. Now or never. "Do you have to be somewhere right now?" she asked. "I mean, do you have time to make another stop?"

Rand turned to face her. *What have you got up your sleeve, Connie?* "I'm free. Where do you want me to drive you?" *Whatever it is I probably need to hear it…and from your lips.*

"Lou Rossi's office."

So that's it. He didn't reply, just checked his mirrors and pulled into traffic.

After several blocks, Connie fingered his sleeve.

He sucked in air. Why had he become so sensitive to her slightest touch?

"Is that where you're driving us?" she asked.

"Yes." He willed himself not to look at her. "I think Rossi's past due for a visit from me—us."

"Do you think he might know something about Troy?" She leaned toward him. "Or am I just grabbing at straws?"

He gripped the steering wheel, unwilling to surrender to his attraction to the warm, caring woman beside him. "I think it's worth our while to ask." *In fact, while I've been waiting for you to decide to do this, I've done my homework on Rossi. But I wanted you with me when I confronted him. Your presence will make Rossi react even if it's negative and that's what I need to see—reactions.*

The large office overlooking the toll road wasn't far, just on the eastern edge of town. Rand parked and walked beside Connie into the building and to Rossi Construction's receptionist desk.

"We don't have an appointment," Connie said to the receptionist. "But I'm a friend of Lou's, Connie Oberlin. Would you ask Uncle Lou if he'll give us a moment of his time?"

The young woman looked them over, but obviously Connie's use of "Uncle" and her professional appearance moved the woman into action. She placed a call and then waved them toward the hallway that led to the office.

Beside his open door, Lou met them in the hallway. The large bear of a man looked worried. "Connie, what is it? Has something else happened?"

"Not to Annie or the boys. No." With lowered gaze, Connie walked into the office and took the seat that Uncle Lou gestured her to.

Rand sat down beside Connie. He'd thought her presence would make this conversation easier but now he wondered if he'd been right. Surely, Rossi wouldn't want to disillusion her.

But it was too late now. They'd come together. "Mr. Rossi, Connie has taken a natural interest in my investigation into your nephew's disappearance."

Lou sat down behind his desk and nodded.

"It has escaped the notice of neither of us that Troy disappeared after leaving your job site." Rand watched for Lou's reaction. "This prompted me to question your employees at Troy's job site—"

"I know. I told them to tell you everything."

Rand tightened his lips. "I'm sure you did. But they may not have witnessed what Troy may have."

Connie shifted restlessly at his side, her sleeve brushed his as she moved her chair slightly.

"I don't get you." Lou picked up a pencil and began doodling circles on his desk pad.

Connie stared at Lou, but remained mute.

Rand took her silence as a request for him to continue. "Or they may not know what you know. Mr. Rossi, is there anything which you haven't told us for any reason that might help us find out what has happened to Troy?"

"I don't know what you mean." Lou stopped doodling and looked up.

Rand fixed the man with an unwavering look. "Was anything illegal happening at the job site? Anything that might have caused your nephew to disappear?"

"Illegal?" Lou's face instantly turned red. "You mean me cutting corners? All my buildings exceed code—"

"No," Rand cut in, "I mean, do you suspect anyone at the site might be dealing drugs, acting as a sheetmaker or runner for a bookie...anything like that?"

"If anything like that is going on, *I* don't know anything about it." Lou belligerently tossed his pencil down to the desk.

"Uncle Lou, this is important. If you know anything, suspect anything, please tell us," Connie's gentle voice coaxed.

Rand watched Connie's words soften the big man.

"I think Troy may have been in debt from gambling," Rand said quietly.

Connie gazed steadily at Rossi.

"How do you get that?" Lou hunched forward, his elbows on the desk top. He suddenly looked older, less imposing.

"I went to the sports bar that Andy and Austin rode the subway to that Saturday morning in June," Rand said. "What they told me afterward about their dad's activities there led me to follow up. It is a place serviced by a bookie's sheetmaker. And he only takes fifty-dollar or higher bets. Nothing small."

"But that doesn't mean Troy was betting too much," Connie objected suddenly.

Rand burned at her ever-ready defense of Troy. But he watched Rossi. "After verifying that Troy could have placed bets at the sports bar, I went back to his job site and questioned his fellow employees and they verified that yes, Troy had been gambling a lot this past year. Something he had rarely done in the past."

Connie looked stunned. Rossi made a sound of disgust.

"This may be all the explanation needed for Troy's disappearance." Rand leaned forward. "But could Troy have seen something, found out something he shouldn't?"

"Not that I know of." Lou tilted back in his high-backed black leather chair.

"It's common knowledge," Rand continued in a voice free of condemnation, "that companies such as yours, construction or waste-hauling, often are targets of extortion. Do you pay protection?" There—he'd said it.

Rossi again shifted in his chair, making the leather squeak. But he said nothing.

His silence was nearly a confession. "I won't ask for facts," Rand proceeded, almost tasting the sour victory. *He's going to open up.* "I just need to know if the mob might be interested in Rossi Construction."

Lou looked at Connie, frowned and glanced back to Rand. "Okay, you're right. I pay protection money. It's just another cost of doing business."

Connie made a little sound, like a strangled groan.

Though Rand had expected it, and even though he sympathized with Connie's disappointment, a surge of bitter triumph galled him.

"The demand for cash comes subtle, you know?" Lou fidgeted with a note pad on his desk. "No one comes right out and tells me I better ante up. I get a call saying that I might want to donate money to a fund. Or sometimes, I just receive calls to send cash to blind post office boxes. Never the same box and never at regular intervals." Rossi held up a hand. "That's all I'm saying and I won't press charges so don't ask me to."

Rand nodded. His suspicion had been proven right, but he didn't feel good about it. Connie had lowered her chin and looked crushed. Rand rose. "We'll leave you then."

"Will this help you find Troy?" Rossi stood also. "I've never had any other connection with the mob in any way. I just pay to protect my workers and my customers' investments. People can do things, set things up on a construction site. People can get hurt, you know? There's no way I can, or the police can, guarantee the safety of my workers if someone decided to hurt them. I don't see that I have a choice in this."

Rand offered Lou his hand. "I understand." In a way, he did. They lived in an evil world. Sometimes a man had to weigh the lesser of two evils. What if Rossi didn't pay the money and as a result, some of his workers died on the job? And in any case, how would Lou Rossi or Rand prove that the calls he received were extortion? And how would Rand proceed against the elusive people behind the calls? It was a crime without fingerprints. *Besides, my job is to find Troy.*

Lou looked relieved. "Remember, I'm not pressing charges and if you try to maneuver me into doing that, I'll forget we ever had this conversation. And Connie is a junior partner in my company's law firm. She must keep what I say to her private."

From under her lashes, Connie stared at Rossi, obviously troubled, hurt.

"Rossi," Rand went on, "do you have any reason to believe that Troy might have been threatened by someone involved in the extortion?"

"No, and I've done some digging myself. No connection."

"Okay then." But what Rossi had said had not surprised Rand that much. He was glad he didn't have to make these kinds of choices. Rand nodded and took Connie's trembling arm. They walked out of the office and its building to Rand's car.

Connie marched beside him as though unaware of the people and cars around her. Unaware of him. He held the door open for her, resisting the urge to run his hand down her arm, reassure her in any way he could. She got in and was so silent, so distant.

He'd gotten used to her insistent presence. He recalled the way she'd stood up to him the night before. How she'd given him comfort when he least deserved it. Now, she began weeping softly beside him.

Why did she have to care so much about another woman's husband? Why did she waste so much effort on Troy? He went around and got in behind the wheel. He put his key in the ignition and drove away. The silence stretched between them. He found himself driving toward his house, which wasn't far from them. He parked in his drive.

"I can't believe it. Uncle Lou—of all people—pays extortion." Connie's voice broke and tears slipped down her cheeks. "I'm finding things out I didn't know about people that I care about. Things I never wanted to know."

"I can understand," Rand said, "your being hurt or angry, but you can't have been this naive. You grew up in a working-class Chicago neighborhood. Why is this hitting you like this?"

"Hearing about it is one thing. But finding out someone like Uncle Lou is actually involved with paying protection is the shocker. It was always out there, not personal."

He understood then. She knew the hard facts of life, but somehow divorced them from her immediate circle. It was just like her not believing that Troy could be in debt to a loan shark. He turned to her. Her crushed expression made him recall all the times she'd rushed to defend Troy.

Then it hit Rand. A gut-wrenching insight slashed through his mind and raw jealousy ripped him in two. "How long have you been in love with Troy Nielsen?"

Chapter Eleven

"I am not in love with Troy." Connie tossed the words back at him.

He opened his door and slammed it. He had to know the truth. "Yes, you are. It's all clear to me now."

Connie climbed out her door and glared at him over the top of his sedan. "You're crazy. Annie's my best friend."

"What does that matter?" He stalked up to the rear of his house and unlocked it, Connie at his heels. "Now I get why you think Troy could do no wrong. You're in love with him."

"Stop saying that. It's *not* true."

He waved her to enter. "Then what is true? Why do you care so much about another woman's husband? Why do you think he can do no wrong?"

Halting inside his back door, she shook her head

at him. "Stop this. We're not going to talk about this. You have no right. I'm leaving."

He moved in front of the door, blocking her. "Yes, we *are* going to talk about this. This is part of my investigation." A frenzied need-to-know took him over. "How do I know you haven't been in touch with Troy? Were…*are* you having an affair with him?"

Connie slapped his face. "You have no right to talk to me like that."

The blow stung his right cheek. "Tell me the truth then. I need to know the truth." *For me, not for the case. For me. I need to know.* He hated making this revealing admission even in silence and only to himself.

"What is it to you?" Breathing fast and flushed, she tried to push past him.

Words failed Rand. But his instincts didn't. He'd wanted to kiss this woman for days, weeks. He wrenched her to him and kissed her.

Connie froze in his arms.

For one incredible moment he was kissing her warm, willing lips.

Then she forced him away. "No."

"Yes." He couldn't stop now. All his senses thrummed to life.

"No. This…everything…the case…it's all too complicated as it is." She pushed her hair back with both hands. "Take me home. Why did you bring me here?"

"I'm sorry." *No, I'm not. I want to kiss you again.*

"You should be." She stood, glaring at him. "You should be very sorry," she repeated.

"I am." *This is crazy.* "Forgive me." *What was I thinking?* "I'll drive you back to the hospital to your car." He pushed open the back door.

"No…I…" She reached for him then, putting her arms around him and laying her head on his shoulder. She choked, fighting sudden tears. "Why did this all have to happen?" Despair laced her voice. "Why is all this happening?"

He let the door shut behind him. His body felt weak with relief. She trusted him and had reached for him.

Rand carefully folded her into his arms. He kissed her hair. *She shouldn't trust me. I can make no guarantees about what may come.* He couldn't say this though, and didn't she already know it?

"This thing with Rossi," he murmured instead, close to her ear, "has upset you, hasn't it?"

"It doesn't fit my life. It feels unreal. Do you understand?" Her lips were so close to his neck, he felt the whisper of their movement.

From his own experience, Rand recalled this same sense of unreality. Last night, he'd felt it for the second time in his life—when he'd gotten the call that his brother had been shot. "I know what you're feeling."

She lifted her lovely face and gazed into his eyes.

"You do, don't you? You know." She breathed in deeply and closed her eyes. "I'm sorry to be so brittle…but can you hold me just a few more minutes? I feel…betrayed, broken inside."

In reply, Rand tightened his hold on her, pulling her flush against his chest. He breathed in her perfume and luxuriated in her smooth hair pressed against his cheek. He'd forgotten what holding a warm woman in his arms felt like. Had it been this intoxicating?

Finally, she murmured, "I didn't expect my first year out of law school to be like this. I never imagined uncovering ugly secrets hidden by people I've known all my life—people I love."

"No one—" he tried to soften his tone for her "—likes to face hard realities about someone they've known and cared about. It's a bitter pill to swallow."

"You're probably right." She inhaled and shook her head as though just awakening. Still, she didn't pull away from him.

"I'm sorry." He stroked her hair, fingering its silken texture. He never let anyone get close enough to touch anymore. He kept to himself, out of range. That must be why this experience was overwhelming his good sense, which insisted he release her now. "I know that it doesn't change anything, but I am sorry."

"You didn't do anything to be sorry for," she absolved him.

"Then why does my cheek still sting?" He tried to lift their mood.

"*That* you deserved. Do you really think that I—"

"No, I don't. I don't know what came over me." His conscience didn't let him off the hook. *It's called jealousy. You don't want to think of this woman loving any other man.* He shook off these unwelcome, impossible thoughts. "You're not the kind of person who would play a friend false."

She leaned her forehead flush against his chin. "Thanks. That means a lot coming from you."

"I guess I find it so unusual," he explained, "for someone to care as much as you do about your friends that I leaped ahead of my…head, my better sense." He wanted her to move away.

He wanted to go on holding her. "I know you'd never behave dishonorably." She wouldn't. Of that he was sure. "That's why you're so upset about old Uncle Lou paying protection and Troy doing things that ended in hurting his wife and boys."

"I hope you're right about me. I don't know what to think about anyone, even myself." She withdrew a bit from him. "I guess it's time I put away childish things like bestowing perfection on those I love. I just never thought believing Troy and Uncle Lou were two of the good guys was being unrealistic."

With his open palm, he rubbed her back, comforting her. The cotton of her blouse molded to her slender form. He felt the strength, the vitality in her. "Even good guys mess up. Perfection is very rare in this world."

"My mind knows that, but my heart didn't."

He grieved for her, for her loss of innocence. *It was bound to happen sometime.* "Unfortunately, both of us chose professions that often bring us into contact with many less than perfect situations and people."

"I guess." She stepped backward, breaking their contact. "What time is it?"

He felt bereft. His arms wanted to reclaim her. He covered this by looking at his watch. "It's only ten to noon." He shoved his hands into his pockets so he wouldn't reach for her again.

Her face dropped. "I better go back to work then."

He smothered an offer to take her to lunch. He had a desk piled high with reports and interdepartmental paperwork to deal with.

And I am treading on dangerous territory with her. I have to be sensible. This case will end and we'll go our separate ways. After a while, we'll just wave at each other when our paths cross. "I'll drive you to your car."

"Thanks. Maybe we can call and check to see how your sister is doing. Maybe you have another niece or nephew already." She smiled at him.

Her smile held such tenderness that all he could do was nod and let her out his door. He watched her walk away from him. Why had he driven her here? *What was I thinking bringing her to my place?* He refused to answer his own question.

* * *

Later that afternoon on the south side of Chicago, Troy huddled at the mouth of the alley and waited. The smell of hot asphalt and his own sweat filled his nostrils. Another sweltering July day. His attention was focused across the street on a phone booth. This phone must be working. Some guy was using it.

In this age of cell phones, Troy hadn't realized that the ordinary sidewalk phone booth had become an endangered species. Either he couldn't find one or all the ones he found had been trashed by vandals. The guy in the booth hung up.

Troy sprinted across the shabby street and slid inside the folding door. He slipped the coins into the slot and dialed the number. His eyes scanned the street watching for anyone taking notice of him.

"Hello?"

It was Annie. The sound of her voice brought moisture to his eyes.

"Annie," he said. The receiver shook in his hand.

"Troy?" Disbelief tightened her voice. "*Troy, where are you?*"

"Annie, I'm so sorry." A sob tried to come up from deep inside him.

"Troy, what happened to you? I've been so worried. Are you all right?"

He heard the tears in her throat. *Oh, Annie, I love you so. I miss you so.* "I'm sorry. I never wanted to put you through this."

"Then *come home*," she pleaded.

"I can't. I can't."

"Why? I need to know what's happened. Are you running from someone, something?"

"I can't explain now, sweetheart. I can't come home now."

"Why not? If you're in trouble, the police can help you—"

"They can't. I just wanted to hear your voice. I had to. How are the twins?"

"How do you think they are?" Annie's voice suddenly sharpened. "How could you run off and leave us like this? I know about the bank accounts. I know about the unpaid bills. How could you, Troy?"

The accusation in her voice shredded what was left of his self-respect. *I am scum.* "I'm sorry. I never meant to hurt you."

"Well, you have," she snapped. "Are you coming home?"

"I can't, Annie. You don't know—"

"I've hired a lawyer." His wife's warm voice had cooled to frigid.

"A lawyer?" His temples pounded. He gagged. "No, Annie—"

"I have grounds for divorce—desertion. And I have to protect myself and our sons. You left a terrible financial mess behind you and my lawyer says we don't know if you've run up debt in other names—"

"Annie, no. I didn't." Tears clogged his throat. "Don't divorce me. Give me a chance."

"Come home and face me."

"I *can't.*"

"Why not?"

"I can't tell you, honey. Just hang in there a little longer," he begged. "I'll get all this straightened out."

"I don't know what you're talking about—"

A computerized voice came on the line, asking for more change.

"Annie, I'm out of change—"

The line went dead in his hands. He hung it up and leaned his head against the cool metal of the phone. Tears washed down his cheeks. *Divorce. She's going to divorce me. Lord, I want to die. I'm so sorry. How can I get out of this mess? I want to die.*

After dropping Connie at her car, Rand had returned to his desk and tunneled deep into his paperwork. Then Annie had phoned to tell him about Troy's call. It had seemed natural for Rand to call and offer to drive Connie to Annie's that night. Again, he wanted to observe Annie's reaction to this development. Perhaps another unrevealed bit of information would be exposed.

And, of course, he wanted to be with Connie again. Had to be near her again. Telling himself he was playing with fire had been futile.

When he'd pulled up in front of Connie's condo,

he'd wondered if they would feel awkward after what had happened between them earlier that day. But Connie had appeared preoccupied, which he could understand. Troy's calling had confirmed his ideas about what had happened to the man. She couldn't be happy about that.

The ride into Chicago had been a silent one, which had only made him more aware of how much the special woman beside him attracted him. But uncertainty gripped him. Connie was giving him no idea what effect the call had had on her. Now with the heat of the July day still in force, the two of them walked from the alley where they'd left Rand's car up the familiar backyard path past the twins' swing set.

Connie paused and touched his arm. "At least we know he's alive. That's good, isn't it?"

What was she expecting him to say? Would Annie and the boys be better off knowing that Troy was alive but refused to come home? He only nodded. Silence was better than empty phrases.

Connie started walking again. Her mind swirled with thoughts and impressions as she walked beside Rand. Troy had called. What had he said? What did it mean? She walked up the back steps with Rand, not knowing what to say to him. Did he feel the same constraint she did after what had passed between them this morning? She shivered in spite of the heat. *Did I really let him kiss me, hold me? I can't let that happen again. We look at life too differently.*

Downstairs, Gracie must have heard them arrive because she came out to them on the porch before Connie had a chance to knock. "We've got the boys down here," Gracie said in a low voice. "Annie wanted to talk to Rand and you without them hearing. Patience and Gil arrived today. They're upstairs with her."

Connie hugged Gracie. Why did it feel like there had been a death in the family and they were planning the wake?

Gracie smiled at Rand and then she crept back into her apartment and quietly closed the door. They mounted the steps. At the top of the stairs, Patience— a pretty blonde—was waiting for them. She stepped back to allow them onto the landing and then embraced Connie.

Connie hugged her back, breathing in her familiar lily of the valley cologne. "I'm so glad you're here."

"Me, too." Patience looked past Connie at Rand. "Gil had a case to finish prosecuting and then we waited until Gil's ex took their son, Darby, for her vacation. They're camping in northern Minnesota near her boyfriend's family. We can stay a week. I can stay longer if I'm needed."

Feeling inexplicably ill at ease, Connie introduced Patience, Annie and Gracie's cousin, to Rand, the man she'd kissed this morning, the man who had accused her of being in love with Annie's husband.

Lord, I don't love Troy, not the way Rand meant. But yes, I still care about Troy. He's still special to me. That's not wrong.

"Patience and Gil married in early June. Gil's a district attorney downstate," Connie explained to Rand as they filed into Annie's living room. Annie sat in an armchair across from Gil, Patience's husband, a lean compact man with glasses and chestnut hair. Connie smiled at him as they sat down on the nearby love seat. Patience sat down beside Gil on the sofa.

"Gil," Connie said, "this is Rand O'Neill—he's been working Troy's case."

"Rand, did you find out anything from the phone company?" Annie asked immediately.

Covertly, Connie scrutinized her. Annie didn't look upset. Her hair was neat and she was wearing the neutral business casual slacks and blouse she must have worn to work at Jack's office today.

"A tracer had been put on your line from day one of the investigation. Troy's call was traced to an outside phone booth on the south side of the city."

"So it took you exactly nowhere," Gil commented.

"Afraid so," Rand admitted. "But I alerted the patrol cops at that precinct so they will be on the lookout for him. I alerted the adjoining precincts also. Troy may be living in that immediate area or somewhere within easy walking distance."

Connie tried to imagine Troy living away from the neighborhood they'd grown up in. She couldn't. She rested her hand on the love seat between Rand and her.

"But didn't you think that Troy might have stolen his truck? Why do you think he's on foot?" Annie asked, leaning forward with her elbows on her thighs.

Rand said, "If Troy has been gambling over his head, he may have stolen his truck and sold it illegally."

"It's so hard to believe we're talking about Troy," Patience said. "I've known him for years. I just can't imagine why he would do that. It's out of character."

Connie shifted on the love seat beside Rand. Maybe one person never could really know another person completely.

Rand glanced at her. "Things happen. People change."

Connie couldn't argue with that.

Across from them, Gil took Patience's hand in his and kissed it. Envy sliced through Connie. Would any man look at her the way Gil was looking at Patience, his bride?

"I told Troy," Annie spoke up, "that I've retained a lawyer and that I'm beginning divorce proceedings."

Her words caught Connie by surprise. "No, Annie." She edged forward.

"I have to protect myself, Connie." Annie drew herself up. "Troy may have run up debt in other names."

"I haven't found any evidence of that as yet," Rand cautioned.

Connie moved her hand closer to him, her fingers ached to fold around his.

"I asked him to come home and together we'd face whatever problems he's gotten into. He wouldn't." Annie looked Connie, and then Patience, in the eye. "I don't even know the man I talked to today—this man who doesn't pay bills, steals his own truck, runs away from his family. I don't know him and I don't want to be married to him."

Something inside Connie constricted, making it hard for her to breathe. *Lord, this can't be happening to my second family, the family you gave me as a gift of love. I don't want to see this happening.* Connie forced air into her tight lungs. "You don't mean that."

"I do. I've been living a lie and I didn't even know it." Annie stood up and began pacing. "Troy and I had problems last year. We went to counseling. I thought we'd gotten to the bottom of things and were getting along fine. We were building trust again or so I thought. How do you think it makes me feel—" Annie turned her back to them, facing out a window "—to know that I've been living in a fool's paradise?"

Connie couldn't move, could barely breathe. The bottom was dropping out of the world she knew, or thought she knew. First Troy's disappearance, then Uncle Lou's guilt and now Annie and divorce. She felt Rand's hand close around hers.

"Annie, why don't you wait until Troy comes home?" Patience suggested, going to stand beside her.

"No, because he might not be coming home." Annie's voice snapped. "I'm not going to tell the boys yet," she said in a low voice. "They don't need to know. With Troy gone, whether we're married or not doesn't really change anything for them. But I've got to get organized to face this. I've got to protect the boys."

Connie couldn't think of a thing to say. The tightness leaked out of her, taking her strength with it. She leaned against Rand's shoulder, so broad, so strong.

Annie glanced around, looking fierce. "Troy's recent behavior has been bizarre. What if he's decided to kidnap them and take them away with him? I just don't trust him anymore. And I wouldn't have a legal leg to stand on to get the twins back unless I'd gotten sole custody. He'd have every right to take them if we're still married. I've got to make sure I've got full custody of them."

Connie closed her eyes.

Rand's cell phone rang, interrupting. He took it out.

"Hey, Rand!" his brother-in-law's voiced burst into his ear. "It's a boy!"

"Great. My congratulations, Larry." He kept Connie's hand in his. "How's my sister?"

"Fine. She came through fine. Our little guy was born about an hour ago. We're still arguing about his name."

Everyone was watching Rand, except for Connie. She stared at her lap. "Good." Rand squeezed Connie's hand. "Say, Larry, I'm sorry, but I'm working now."

"Okay. Just wanted you to hear the good news."

"Thanks." Rand snapped his phone shut.

Rand made himself smile at the faces turned to him. "My sister Molly had a baby boy an hour ago."

"I'm glad," Connie said softly, looking into his eyes.

He wanted to kiss her, but didn't.

Annie burst into tears, her new self-reliance collapsing from within. "Maybe this is all my fault. Maybe if I'd postponed school and gotten pregnant last year like Troy wanted me to, none of this would have happened."

"Don't start that pointless exercise." Rand rose, letting go of Connie. "Annie, I've seen other people waste emotion on that. Don't play the what-if game." *I did it over Cara.* "It doesn't help. None of us knows why people do the things they do. All that might have been different is that you would have been left alone to take care of three children instead of two."

No one made a reply.

Connie looked up at him.

He offered her his hand. He wanted out of here now. "Connie, I want to go to the hospital and see my new nephew through the glass." *Come with me,* he silently urged.

She surprised him. She rose without objecting. "I think I will go with you. Annie, you have Patience here."

"Sure. You've been great, Connie, but I've got to get over this leaning on everyone." Annie wiped her tears with her hands. "I can take care of myself, of the boys. I have to."

Goodbyes were said and Rand and Connie left Annie in Patience and Gil's care. After a silent ride, Rand parked the car in the hospital parkade and led Connie into the elevator and up to the maternity ward. The muffled cries of newborns greeted them. He'd been there often enough as his younger siblings had begun their families. At the brightly lit window looking into the nursery, a gaggle of his family had congregated.

Connie halted and pulled back from him. "Oh, I shouldn't have come. I didn't realize your whole family might be here."

At the same moment, Chuck—his arm in a sling—caught sight of them. "Hey! It's Rand and Connie." A shy Sheila stood at his side.

Rand gritted his teeth. Why hadn't he anticipated this welcoming committee, either?

"Oh, Connie, come and see our newest little one,"

his mother invited. "We're just about to go home. I'm beat after chasing this little girl all day."

Molly's daughter Alexa was perched high in her grandfather's arms. "New brother," she said, pointing to the nursery window.

The O'Neill family all beamed and "awwed" in approval.

Rand and Connie were shunted to the front of the group right in front of the glass. Chuck pointed out the correct isolette and Rand gazed at the blue-wrapped and knit-capped bundle. An odd feeling snaked through him—a happy sadness. A baby. Another innocent.

"He's adorable," Connie murmured.

Rand found the expression on her face irresistible. She would make a lovely mother.

"Eight pounds, seven ounces, twenty-one inches long," the proud grandmother announced. "Now, Connie, you must come to his christening. Our family always has the newborn christened on the Sunday after the mother comes home from the hospital. I'll be hosting the party."

Rand clenched his jaw. His family knew nothing of subtlety.

"That's very kind of you, but—"

"No buts about it," Chuck put in. "You're my rescuer and you have to come."

"Yes, please come," Molly said. Wearing a shapeless cotton hospital gown and robe, she stood in the doorway beside the nursery window. "I'd love to have you. Please."

Connie looked to Rand. He shrugged. She sighed and capitulated. "All right."

Rand's family voiced their joy and then began talking to Molly. Rand pulled Connie out of the cluster of his siblings, their spouses and children. "I'm taking Connie home. She's had a long day."

Another round of family goodbyes and then once again, Connie sat beside him in his car. His keen awareness of her overwhelmed him, making it hard to draw a deep breath.

"I'm sorry if my family railroaded you into that," he apologized.

"It's all right. You have a nice family."

"Most people think so." He started the car and drove into the deep twilight.

Connie chuckled softly.

The sound danced through him. *What am I going to do with you, Connie?*

Too soon, he was in front of her condo. Without a word, he got out and escorted her to her door.

They stood facing each other on her front step. Moments passed. She didn't make a move to go in. He didn't turn to go to his car.

He opened his arms and she walked into them. He held her close, letting the sensation of having her so near sink deep inside his consciousness, gentle summer rain on his parched heart. Holding her felt so right.

She lifted her head as if asking for a kiss.

He bent and covered her soft mouth with his.

She responded to his caress. Breath fluttered from her, warming his face. He kissed her again, deepening and savoring the feeling, the taste of her.

He lifted his face from hers to look at her. "You're letting me kiss you."

"Yes. You're kissing me."

"After all, why shouldn't we?" he asked. A thousand reasons flocked together in his mind. He shut the door on them all.

"Why shouldn't we?" she repeated.

"Let's not think about that now," he urged, holding reality at bay.

"I'm tired of thinking," she agreed. She initiated another kiss. Her soft lips moving under his.

Only one thought came through his mind clearly—*Thank You, God.*

Chapter Twelve

Late on a Sunday afternoon, Connie stood near the cluster of Rand's family, including a blushing Sheila at Chuck's side. All dressed in their Sunday best, they'd gathered in the small chapel off the large sanctuary. A stained-glass window picturing Christ's own baptism and the white dove from heaven took up most of one wall. The bright blue-and-red glass gleamed in the summer sunlight, glimmering over the white walls and aged oak floor.

Connie had passed his family's church many times in Taperville. It was one of the original churches—a large two-story red brick, imposing and solid—in the old part of the little town which over the past decade had finally succumbed to Chicago's urban sprawl.

She'd tried to get out of coming, but Rand had explained that she'd get more attention from his "helpful" family if she didn't show. They would all want to know why. She had capitulated and now tried to make herself as inconspicuous as she could. In an attempt to be a chameleon, she'd worn an off-white summer sheath, matching low heel pumps and no jewelry. She stood with her arms at her sides, a half step behind Rand.

In a dark, well-cut suit, Rand stood protectively close to her, his shoulder against hers. Over a week had passed since Troy's phone call, a period of upheaval. His nearness had become such a solace to her. They'd spent each evening together. Rand surreptitiously enclosed her hand in his.

His rough palm warmed her cold hand. She couldn't help it. Her low spirits lifted. She and Rand had been together some part of every day since Troy's phone call. *What's going on with Rand and me, Lord? We never talk about it. It's just...we need to be near each other.* Would their relationship vanish if they talked about it? Did they *have* a relationship?

The minister, wearing his white and gold-trimmed Sunday vestments, cleared his throat.

Connie turned her dark thoughts to the bright occasion at hand. Molly cradled and cooed to her infant son while her husband Larry held their two-year-old daughter. The little family couldn't have looked happier if they'd tried. A real Kodak moment.

"I think we can begin now." After a brief prayer,

the pastor lifted his open black leather Bible and began to read: " 'Some people brought children to Jesus to place His hands on them, but the disciples scolded the people.

" 'When Jesus noticed this, He was angry and said to His disciples, "Let the children come to Me, and do not stop them, because the Kingdom of God belongs to such as these. I assure you that whoever does not receive the Kingdom of God like a child will never enter it." Then Jesus took the children in His arms, placed hands on each of them, and blessed them.' "

The pastor looked up and smiled. "That is why Christ told Nicodemus, 'You must be born again.' We must put away our scornful worldly wisdom if we are to see with the eyes of faith, to see clearly God's love for us in this dark, wicked age. Today, through faith, we believe that Jesus is here with us and He is blessing—with light and life—this little child who has been brought to Him. Who are the godparents?"

One of Rand's younger sisters and her husband stepped forward. "We are Jackson Trevor's godparents."

The pastor spent a few moments impressing upon the young couple the responsibilities that a godparent assumes. They both gave their assurances that they were aware of the duties and were committed to fulfilling them.

Then the pastor took little Jackson Trevor into his

arms and said a prayer. From the baptismal font, he poured a trickle of water over the baby's head and intoned, "In the name of the Father, the Son and the Holy Spirit, I baptize thee, Jackson Trevor, into Christ Jesus, our Lord and Savior."

The baby opened his eyes and gave the pastor a pointed how-dare-you look. The O'Neill family laughed and "awwed" over the baby just like at the nursery window. The solemn moment gave way to joy.

Rand gripped Connie's hand more tightly in his. She returned the reassuring pressure and blinked away tears. Was she crying over this touching occasion? Or over the past or was it her future? She felt shame that she was making herself the focus of what had happened to Annie and Troy. *I know it isn't about me, Lord. But I care so much. I hurt so much....*

The baptism accomplished, digital cameras appeared in numerous hands. Connie and Rand fled, as of one accord, to the rear fringe of the family. Chuck held Sheila in the thick of things and she blushed through many photos. Holding hands, Connie and Rand watched the flurried activity but managed not to draw anyone's attention.

"Rand," Dorcas called finally, "bring Connie over here for a photo. We're about done. But I want the two of you holding Jackson Trevor."

Her pulse zooming, Connie pulled away from Rand and stepped backward farther into the afternoon shadows near the door. "No, sorry, I—"

"Don't be camera-shy," Dorcas insisted. "It will only sting a little."

"Ha, ha," Rand replied. "Connie and I aren't ready to appear together *digitally*—as yet."

Dorcas frowned and shook her head. She turned away and then swung back and snapped a photo of them. "Gotcha!"

Connie's face flamed. She opened her mouth, ready to babble something like, "We're just friends." But wisely, she closed her mouth without speaking.

Rand rubbed her back in a comforting way. "I'm hungry," he said in a loud voice. "Haven't you tortured little Jackson Trevor enough by now? He's been passed around so many times he must feel like a football in the final quarter of play."

Connie sighed silently. She appreciated Rand's take-charge use of humor. She liked his family, but every time they saw her with Rand they tried to make Rand and her into a couple. At some level, she sensed she didn't understand or want to explore, it saddened her that they weren't really a couple. *I just need to be near him now. I can't say it any other way.*

As Rand escorted Connie out the side door of the church into the sleepy hot Sunday afternoon, he wished his family would lay off. Couldn't he and Connie just enjoy being together without everyone making it such a big deal? He could answer that. Of course, they couldn't. His family naturally behaved as though he and Connie were engaged. *We aren't even formally dating.*

Once more his conscience stung him. *You've spent every evening together since that drive into Chicago over Troy's phone call. If you're not dating, what are you doing?*

I'm spending time with a woman who makes me feel...quiet, peaceful...renewed. He heard the pastor's voice again—"I assure you that whoever does not receive the Kingdom of God like a child will never enter it." Why had that come to mind?

The post-christening party—complete with good food, delicious cake and lots of O'Neill laughter—was still going strong at Rand's parents' home when Rand drew Connie outside into the deep lavender twilight. "Let's leave."

She looked up at him. He saw the relief in her brown eyes. "I should say goodbye to your parents and thank them—"

"They'll just try to take another photo of us. Let's go. I'll make amends later."

Fingering his collar, straightening it unnecessarily, Connie looked at him and then nodded. "Okay."

He caught her hand and would have kissed it, but stopped himself. They were too exposed here. Too many eyes longed to see any exchange of affection between Connie and him.

He led her outside and then around the garage to

his car. After a quiet ride to Connie's condo, he parked in the drive and got out and followed her.

"It's been a lovely day," Connie offered as she approached her door.

Would she ask him in?

She unlocked the door, walked in and held the door open for him to follow her.

Silent relief sighed through him. She was granting him a few more prized minutes of her company. He realized he'd come to live from one interlude with her to the next. Everything else in his life was mere static. He took off his sports jacket and put it on the back of one of the kitchen stools at the bar. "Ah."

She smiled at him. "I want to get out of my stockings and these heels." She shuffled up her stairs.

Connie's condo still smelled of new carpeting and drywall. He liked the semi-decorated look of it. Connie's life had just begun. She hadn't had time to fill it up. He'd lived almost fifteen years longer and was tired of much of what cluttered his life. Too much past…

Shutting down this avenue of thought, Rand walked over and opened the slider to her patio. Another storm had gone through last night and leached all the humidity out of the summer air. He stood gazing at the row of condos behind Connie's with their high-fenced patios. Voices and snatches of music floated on the breeze.

Connie came up behind him. She'd changed into

a long casual blue plaid cotton dress and her feet were bare. "A lovely evening."

As though he'd been doing it for years, he turned and took her into his arms. He buried his face in her neck, breathing in her subtle fragrance.

She kissed his forehead as if bestowing a benediction and lifted her fingers through his hair. He shuddered at her gentle touch.

Then she drew him back inside to her love seat where she relaxed against him and he put his arm around her shoulders. With his palm, he turned her face toward him and kissed her lips. She kissed him back, her lips caressing his, and then she pulled away and rested her head on his shoulder. They gazed out as night crept in. Patio lights flickered on one by one and fireflies glimmered on and off.

This was the way they had spent the end of each evening together. Just a peaceful time of being together, neither pushing to speak or move the relationship to another level. It was enough to just be together, enough just to hold the warmth and softness of her in his arms.

Did she expect him to say anything? Did she expect him to tell her how he felt about her? *How do I feel about you, Connie?* The answer came immediately—*I can't let you go.*

He tried to make sense of what he was feeling, what he should say. "Connie, I—"

Her phone rang, shattering their tranquility. As though she dreaded responding to it, Connie hesitated, arching against him, her head turned toward the phone. But when the answering machine picked up, Gracie's voice came loud and clear in the silent room. "Connie, if you're there, pick up. They've found Troy! They're taking him to Cook County hospital."

Connie shot up and raced to the phone. "Gracie! I'm here."

"Come, we need you. Come. Please." Gracie was weeping.

"What happened to him?"

"They didn't tell us. We're leaving now." Gracie moaned.

"We'll be right there." Connie turned.

But Rand had shut the patio door and was already donning his sports coat. "Let's go."

Rand and Connie hurried into the busy E.R. It smelled of strong disinfectant. Keeping Connie close to his side, Rand showed his badge to the receptionist. "We're here about Troy Nielsen. I've been working his missing person's case." The receptionist motioned them down the corridor to their right. They followed her directions and stepped to the hall outside an examining area.

The knot of horror-struck family—Annie, Gracie and Jack—were clustered there. Beyond them, a doctor and nurse hovered over an obviously homeless man who lay on the examining table.

"Troy," Connie gasped, bumping into Rand's shoulder.

A police officer, standing at the opening, moved forward to stop Connie from intruding. Rand flashed his badge. He offered the cop one of his hands and with the other took hold of Connie's elbow. "I've been handling Troy Nielsen's missing person's case. What's happened?"

"I'm a patrol officer on the south side." The cop was older than Rand and rugged looking. "I was making my rounds when I heard sounds of a fight, or maybe a beating would be a better description. My partner and I sped up the alley and surprised three perps beating the…the stuffing out of this guy. When they saw our car, they scattered. But I've seen them before. They're enforcers for a couple of loan sharks." He nodded toward the bed. "Looks like he missed a payment or two."

Rand watched Connie absorb this as if it had been a physical blow. He firmed his grip on her arm. "How is Nielsen?"

The doctor turned to answer Rand. "He's a mess, but nothing life-threatening. Just multiple lacerations and contusions. I don't think he's suffered a concussion or any internal injuries apart from a few cracked or bruised ribs. I will do a few X rays just to be sure. But if those are all right, he can go home and get a shower and a meal. He looks like he needs both badly."

Rand scanned the group in the hall. All appeared to be in the throes of horror and shock. Connie stood beside him paralyzed. He ached with the disagreeable sensation of being proved right when he'd have rather been wrong.

"I'll need Nielsen," the cop spoke up, "to answer some questions when he's able to talk and if he wants to get the ones who did this to him, he'll have to come down and press charges. We'll need descriptions, too."

"No." The crumpled bloody form in the bed croaked this one word. "No charges."

The cop drew nearer Troy. "You may want to think that over. If we hadn't shown up when we did, you could have ended up a pile of hamburger. They probably wouldn't have killed you but they might have broken a leg or arm or one of each. What's a guy with a nice family like you have, hanging around with…that kind…getting in this kind of mess?"

Rand came closer to the cop, Connie still beside him. "I'll be staying with Nielsen and I'll make sure he gets home. Why don't you give me your card and I'll make sure he gets back to you?"

The cop nodded, gave Rand his card and left. Nielsen was rolled past Rand and Connie on his way to X-ray.

Rand gazed down at him—two swollen weepy eyes, a split lip, bruised jaw. Troy Nielsen wasn't a pretty sight and it would only be worse tomorrow. But Rand couldn't dredge up much sympathy for him. The guy had screwed up royally and put his family through hell.

It was nearly midnight. Supporting Nielsen by the arm, Rand followed Connie up the back steps to Annie's apartment without a word. Troy was weaving and unsteady. Rand gripped him tightly. *You're not getting away from me again, pal.*

"Hurting my arm," Troy mumbled, trying to pull away.

Rand gripped him tighter. "Stop it. You'll fall down the stairs and have to go back to the hospital."

They made it into the apartment. Annie, grim-faced, met them in the kitchen. "The boys are downstairs asleep. I didn't want them to hear or see this. Patience is there, too." She pointed to the spare bedroom. "Take him in there."

Connie took a step toward her friend. "Annie—"

"Need a shower," Troy mumbled again.

"I'll take care of it," Rand said, pushing the man into the small bathroom. "Bring me some clean clothes for him."

Connie followed him with her eyes.

With one last look at her, Rand shut the door and made quick work of stripping Troy's filthy clothing off, helping him into the shower, and turning on the hot water. Steam rose in the room.

A knock sounded. Rand opened the door and Annie handed him folded underwear, pajamas and a robe for Troy. He handed her the rags at his feet. "Put these in a trash bag and take them directly outside to the garbage cans now."

Within a half hour, Troy, in his pajamas and robe, Rand, Connie and Annie sat around the kitchen table. His hand shaking, Troy was sipping a glass of milk. "It's good to be home."

Annie stared at her husband. "You can stay here tonight, but tomorrow you better go to your mother's."

"Annie, I'm sorry—"

"What did you do, Troy?" Annie's voice cracked like a whiplash. "Detective O'Neill says you were in debt to bookies. Is he right? Were you gambling?"

Troy nodded.

"Why? Whatever possessed you to do that?" Annie demanded.

Rand let Annie take the lead. He would just listen and take mental notes.

Sitting like a stick figure, Connie was watching without an expression or word.

"It—I started last summer when…we were having problems," Troy said.

"*Don't* you *dare* try to blame this on my going back to school." Annie leaned forward, her chin jutting out.

"Not." Troy shook his head and then grimaced with the pain of the movement. "Just went to this sports bar with one of the guys from work. He placed a bet and so I did too. Won. Won several times and then I started losing."

"Why didn't you tell me?" Annie lashed out again.

"Couldn't. Knew you'd be mad. Thought I could win big and pay off." He hung his head and mumbled, "Didn't."

Why didn't people understand that the bookie or the casino always won in the end? Rand looked away.

Connie was staring at her hands, hunched over.

"Then I started betting way too much." Troy's voice strengthened. "Don't know why. You came back. Everything should have gone fine. But I couldn't stop." A note of desperation vibrated in the man's voice.

The same old story. Gambling could become an addiction. How many sorry souls had found out that awful truth?

"Couldn't pay up. Had to borrow money from a loan shark. Then couldn't pay him so borrowed from another to pay the first."

Rand closed his eyes. What a mess.

Connie shook her head but in slow motion.

"*Why* didn't you tell me?" Tears hovered in the back of Annie's accusation. "We could have worked this out, borrowed money, paid off the debt."

"Couldn't stop betting. Tried." Troy hung his head. "Couldn't. Thought you'd be better off without me—"

"Oh, yes," Annie began to deal out the sarcasm, "you've ruined our credit rating, broken your sons' hearts, shamed your parents and nearly destroyed our marriage. Your leaving accomplished a lot."

Troy put down the empty milk glass on the table-top. "I'll find a way to…pay them, get them off…our backs. I'll make it up to you. Promise."

One tear trickled down Connie's cheek.

Feeling his chest expanding with dread, Rand intervened. "I'm going to put him to bed before he collapses and I have to carry him."

Annie looked disgusted and waved toward the guest room. She turned to her friend. "Connie, Patience is sleeping downstairs, helping Gracie keep an eye on the boys. I hate to ask you, but will you stay with me? I don't want to be alone with…*him*."

Rand helped Troy up and let him lean against him as he led him into the darkened room and onto the open sofa bed. Troy moaned as he lay down.

"Those cracked ribs will give you grief for quite a while." Rand found a bit of sympathy for Troy. He'd committed all the mistakes Annie had enumerated, but he'd paid an awful price over the past months and especially tonight. He'd been beaten by experts and Rand had no doubt that he would have suffered a broken arm or leg or worse if the police hadn't broken up the beating. Enforcers sent a message to others who might welsh on their debts.

Connie was waiting for Rand as he came out. Annie must have gone to bed. "I need to stay." Her voice was flat.

"I know." He tried to read her expression, but

could not. He wanted to take her into his arms, but she gave him no sign that this would be welcome. "I'll see you tomorrow."

"Thanks, Rand, for everything." Her voice held some quality, some message he couldn't decipher.

Was she just saying thanks, or goodbye to him?

Unnerved, he waved and walked down the back steps. *I'll ask her tomorrow. I'll take her aside and...*

As he reached the lower hallway that opened to the porch and Gracie's back door, he heard voices. Gracie and Jack had left their door ajar. He moved forward to say good-night and to pull their door shut.

"Dad, I can't believe Troy ended up like this," Gracie said.

"When a man leaves the straight and narrow path," Mike Petrov replied, "anything can happen. I just hope Annie and he can put this right. I don't want them to divorce unless Troy persists in gambling. Then she'd have no choice."

Rand paused. When had Mike come?

"I'm not so worried about Annie," Gracie insisted. "I think she's matured, had to mature to face this."

"You're right," Mike agreed, "She's made me proud."

"Me, too." Gracie's voice lowered. "But it's Connie I'm worried about."

"You mean her old infatuation with Troy?" Mike asked. "Do you think she still has feelings for him?"

Rand stopped breathing.

"Yes," Gracie said, "I can't forget that Connie was very much in love with Troy—"

"But that was years ago," Mike said dismissively. "Long before Annie and Troy even dated."

"I know. I don't think Connie is still in love with him really. But you can't deny that she has always had a special feeling for him."

"Always put him on a pedestal, you mean?" Mike asked.

Rand felt sick as he heard his own thoughts confirmed by people who would know, who'd known Connie most of her life.

"Yes," Gracie said, "and he has fallen off now—"

Rand let himself out the back door. Somehow he stumbled his way to his car and got in. He sat staring at the darkened dashboard.

I'm not in love with Troy—Connie had tossed that declaration at him just days ago. He still believed her. Their wanting to be together, all they'd shared over the past week and more had proved she had feelings for *him.* But had she left behind all her feelings for Troy? Was she ready to move on?

His heart hurt as though someone had jabbed it. And he finally could admit it. *I'm in love with you, Connie. I'm ready to move on with my life—to finally put the past behind me. But are you, Connie, or are we doomed to always be out of step?*

Chapter Thirteen

On Tuesday morning, Connie sat in a corner conference room at her law office. Sunshine glinted off the brass eagle on top of the American flag at the front of the room. Floyd Sanders was across from her, smoothing back his thinning hair. Tomorrow was the day to plead his arson case before a judge, to do what she'd been hired to do. What she didn't think she could do.

The silent maple-paneled room felt like a yawning cavity. "Mr. Sanders, I've beat the bushes for expert witnesses to shore up your defense. I haven't found any. The insurance company will testify against you. The state fire marshal will testify against you. The local fire chief and a few of his firefighters will testify against you."

"What about Cudahy? His testimony will make the jury doubt. That's all I need—a reasonable doubt."

Connie held back scalding words she wanted to fling at her client. "Ed Cudahy's landlady told me something that has made me suspicious about his veracity."

"What do you mean?" Floyd Sanders scowled at her.

"I mean Ed Cudahy suddenly had a large amount of cash to flash around…just after he talked to you."

"That doesn't mean a thing. How could they prove I paid him?" Sanders became belligerent. "Huh? How?"

"Very simple." Connie felt her face freeze into a painful smile. "The district attorney's office would only have to interview Mr. Cudahy's landlady and hear what I heard from her. After that conversation, I suspected him of being suborned, so why wouldn't they?"

"How could they prove I paid him?" he repeated.

Dread wedged sideways in Connie's throat. "If this goes to a jury, they wouldn't have to *prove* it, they could just give their reasoning by subpoenaing the landlady and questioning her on the stand. That would put doubt in the jury's mind." *And I don't want Ed Cudahy to be in danger of a perjury charge.*

Without warning, her mind dragged her away from her present suffering. Images flashed of a coolly restrained Rand; a battered, bleeding and filthy Troy in the emergency room; and then the way Annie had looked at her husband with unabashed scorn…

Her mind was a fuzzy ball of angora.

A knock on the door and Grove entered.

Cold panic started in the pit of her stomach. What did he want?

"Ah, Miss Oberlin, I thought you were in here with Mr. Sanders. We've just received a call from the assistant district attorney."

"The assistant district attorney?" Her throat tried to close up after speaking these words.

"Yes, he's on his way here. He has a deal to offer our client."

"What kind of deal?" Sanders barked. "I've got a witness—"

"Please, Mr. Sanders," Grove said. "We can at least hear the man out. If this can be settled out of court, all the better."

Sanders scowled at them both.

"I'll send someone in with coffee for you and we've got some delicious sweet rolls today," Grove said placatingly. "Miss Oberlin, I'd like to have a moment of your time on another matter."

Caught between remaining with Floyd Sanders and going with Grove, Connie felt her unpleasant options closing in on her.

By Grove's side, she walked down the corridor, feeling oddly separate from the office activity around her. He motioned her into his office and closed the door behind them. They both sat down, facing each other, his desk between them.

He cleared his throat. "I decided I needed to give you a little guidance. I think I know—without your saying anything—what you're up against trying to defend Sanders. The man seems to enjoy toeing the edge of the law—if you get my drift. Anyway, that makes him a frequent client, but perhaps this time…"

Grove paused. "I went a little hard on you over that other matter we discussed. So if you don't mind, I'll try to help you out with this. I think a plea bargain could save everyone, including Sanders, a lot of unnecessary trouble."

So he regretted coming down hard on her about her invading Lou's files. Still, Connie didn't trust her voice. She nodded.

"I've tried to think why the D.A. would make Sanders an offer and I can only come up with the fact that they may see it as a slam dunk and have other cases piling up. The insurance company isn't likely to pay Sanders' claim. They need only cite the state fire marshal's report—"

A knock on the door.

"Come in." Grove stood up.

Maureen opened the door. "The assistant district attorney."

A lawyer, only a few years older than Connie, walked in. After introductions and a few moments of polite greeting, the assistant district attorney opened the topic on all their minds. "We don't think Sanders can win and we don't want to waste a judge and court time on an easy case. If your client pleads no contest, we will give him the minimum jail time and fine."

"Jail time?" Connie felt the strength from her drain down to her feet. Sanders would never go for that.

"I don't think a businessman of Sanders's stature in the community," Grove replied, "ought to have to do jail time. Especially when he hasn't pled guilty and you haven't proved your case."

"Exactly," Connie managed to say.

"Arson is a serious crime." The A.D.A. frowned. "Arson for profit is sleazy and dangerous." He recounted some of the conflicting evidence about where the fire at the warehouse had originated and then he touched on the evidence supporting the presence of an accelerant. Finally he ended with, "Someone could have gotten hurt."

"But no one was hurt," Connie said.

"And again I don't think Sanders will get the insurance money," Grove added. "So he will not be profiting from arson in any case."

"That's one reason why our office is making this offer." The opposing counsel folded his hands in front of his chin. "But he cost the city money for the firefighters and he put them in danger. That's why we insist on jail time."

Grove looked at her. It was easy to read his face. It said plainly, *Take it. This is as good as a deal as Sanders is going to get.*

After that, everything went quickly. At first, Floyd Sanders balked at accepting the deal. Privately, Grove explained to him the firm's concerns about going to trial, the overwhelming evidence against him, and why he would most likely fare worse in court. Floyd Sanders glared at her through the whole exchange, but he didn't argue with Grove. And in the end, he accepted the plea bargain.

When she communicated this to the A.D.A. in Grove's office, Connie had a hard time meeting the man's eyes. She felt that Sanders's guilt had smeared her reputation along with his own. After Grove and the A.D.A. had left, she went back to Sanders, who glared at her and called her several ugly names under his breath.

"You're free until sentencing," Connie said, not looking at him. She shoved her yellow legal pad into her briefcase and snapped it shut.

"This is all *your* fault," Sanders exhorted in a nasty tone. "You didn't do a thing for me. I might as well have done without a lawyer."

"*I* certainly would have preferred that." She turned toward the door.

Sanders grabbed her by the arm. "You think you're too good for me. That's why you did such a lousy job. I've seen the way you look at me—like I crawled out from under a rock."

Connie pulled from his grasp and opened the door.

"You'll pay for this," Sanders hissed. "I'm not

going to jail when this is *all your fault!*" Then he charged past her, nearly knocking her aside.

Back in her own office, Connie dialed a number. When the other party picked up, she said, "Mr. Cudahy, this is Mr. Sanders's lawyer. The case is over. Mr. Sanders accepted a plea bargain. You won't have to testify."

"Do I have to give his money back then?" The older man sounded confused.

Connie closed her eyes, thankful that neither the assistant district attorney nor a judge had ever had access to this poor man. "No, you don't. Mr. Cudahy, don't ever do anything like this again. You could have ended up in jail for perjury."

"Oh."

Connie hung up after saying goodbye. *I give up, Lord. I don't know where You want me to be, what You want me to do. Nothing has gone right since I left law school.*

Then Rand's face came to mind. She closed her eyes with the sharp pang he brought to her. Their association was over now. Troy had been found. Rand had been right all along and she had been an idealistic fool.

Her eyes burned from lack of sleep. Every night when she went to bed, closing her eyes opened an internal debate. One part of her recited Troy's sins against Annie and his sons. The other part tried to soften the implications.

But she knew that the second was the dishonest voice, not the voice of her conscience. *Lord, how did this all happen? How could Troy have strayed so far from what I believed him to be?*

Her conscience chimed in, *Why does it matter what you believed him to be? He's Annie's husband. And he's just a man. Why did you think he was so special, so different?*

The answer to that question was too painful, but it came anyway. *A part of me still clung to what I felt and thought about him when we dated in high school.*

High school, her conscience taunted, *how long ago was* that? *Grow up.*

Hot tears blinded her. She leaned her forehead into her hand, trying to imagine never resting her head on Rand's broad shoulder, never again feeling his strong, caring arms banded around her.

"Witch," the voice on the phone snarled that evening. "You didn't do anything to help me win my case. I had to do everything—"

"Mr. Sanders, I'm going to hang up now and do not call me again here or in the office." Connie hung up, but her heart jumped like someone on a trampoline.

"I'm not going to go to jail!" Sanders raved over Connie's phone Wednesday evening, calling her a string of insults. "I'm getting a new lawyer and I'm going to sue you! You're not getting off scot-free."

Connie hung up and then disconnected the phone from the wall. She paced around her kitchen, clenching and unclenching her hands.

Late on Thursday night, Connie listened to her phone ring and ring. It finally stopped. Within minutes, it started again. This had gone on for nearly an hour.

Fear and anger contending inside her, Connie moved so that she was standing right over the phone. When it stopped ringing, she counted one-two and then lifted it up. Dial tone. The sickening fear that Floyd Sanders was actually capable of hiring someone to hurt her triumphed. *I have to do something.*

She quickly tapped in the number of the Taperville police station. "Chuck O'Neill, please."

She was transferred to him. She closed her eyes and took a deep breath. "Chuck, this is Connie. I've got a problem."

"Hi, big brother," Chuck said into his desk phone.

"Yeah," Rand replied.

"Don't sound so friendly. I might think you know me," Chuck teased.

"What do you want?" Rand barked. "I'm off duty tonight."

"I'm on duty, but I've got a job you should take care of."

"What is it?"

"Connie's being harassed," Chuck said, his voice serious now, "by phone."

Silence.

"Who is it?" Rand asked.

"It's her client. He's been calling and abusing her every evening since he had to take a plea bargain on Tuesday."

"That's something you should handle—" Rand started to hang up.

"No, it's something *you've* got to handle. She's scared. Really scared he might hire someone to hurt her. Don't you care?"

"Why…I…" Rand's voice faded into nothingness. "Okay. When did she report this?"

"Just a few minutes ago. I told her we'd get right on it."

Rand hung up.

"You're welcome, big brother." Chuck sat back in his chair and grinned. "Just don't screw this up."

Rand parked his car in Connie's drive. He stared at her windows concealed with blinds and her locked door—a fortress armed against him. *Why did Chuck call me?* But Rand knew the answer to that. And he knew why he'd come to. He opened his car door and got out.

Chapter Fourteen

Rand stood at Connie's door. *I have a job to do. I'm here to help her.* But he admitted that he wanted to be here, had wanted to be with Connie since that awful night Nielsen had been found. Would Connie welcome him? Or did she want nothing further to do with him now that Troy was back?

The conversation he'd overheard between Gracie and her dad had kept him awake nights, had kept him away. Was it true or false? Finally he made himself knock. While he waited, his heart seemed to swell to twice its size.

The door was opened with caution. Connie stood in the doorway, staring out at him. The mournful look in her eyes made it hard for him to swallow. She didn't speak, either, merely stepped back to let him enter.

He walked inside the home that he'd felt so comfortable in just days ago. Had it really been just days since he'd held this silent woman? Now, it was if he were walking onto uncharted land. He paused by the kitchen bar. He cleared his throat. "You've been getting calls?"

"Oh, did Chuck send you?" She sounded disappointed.

Maybe she'd wanted Chuck to come, not him. He steeled himself against this thought. "Yes, Chuck said I should take care of this. That you'd feel more comfortable talking to me than a stranger." Though he knew the exact opposite was probably true.

"You came about the phone calls?" she asked as if he had been speaking in a riddle.

He wished he could tell her the truth—that he'd come because he'd grabbed at any excuse for coming, for being here with her once more. *Connie, I want to be near you, hold you once more.* But would this be the last time they were together?

The shaft of fiery pain that shot through his heart nearly made him gasp. He steadied himself with a hand on the kitchen bar. "When did this start?"

"I'm sure it's my client—my former client, Floyd Sanders. He accepted a plea bargain on Tuesday morning. He called me that night. He used vulgar insults. But I thought…he was just angry, that he would be smart enough not to call again after I hung up on him. But then he called the next evening…and he threatened me. I recorded him on my answering machine."

He had the sudden urge to find Sanders and put his hands around the creep's throat. Instead, after years of routine investigations, Rand pulled out his note pad and pen. "What form did the threat take?"

"I beg your pardon?"

"What did he threaten to do to you?"

"Nothing specific." She looked down. "Just that 'I'd pay.'"

He nodded, preparing his constricted throat for speech. "Did he call again tonight?"

"Yes. At least, I think it's him. Someone just keeps calling, letting it ring and ring. I haven't answered."

As if on cue, the phone began ringing. Rand strode over and picked up. "Rand O'Neill for Connie Oberlin."

Breathing on the line.

"I'm a detective with the Taperville force. *What* do you want?"

The line clicked. Dial tone.

He hung up, disappointed. He'd had several comments he'd wanted to make to the jerk. "That may take care of it. If he thinks the police have a personal…interest in your safety, he may drop it."

"If it doesn't—" She still wouldn't meet his eyes.

"I think it will." A fierce protectiveness rushed through him. *Connie, I would do anything to keep you safe.*

Don't leave me, Rand. Connie could feel these words forming deep in her throat. She swallowed trying to hold them back. *He was just investigating Troy's disappearance. And he was right all along and I wouldn't listen. I was such a fool. He doesn't want me.*

Really? her inner voice countered. *Is that why just days ago he held you in his arms in this very room?*

It didn't mean anything to him. He never said anything.

Did you say anything? the voice chided.

I couldn't. He didn't want me to. I didn't want to.

Rand tucked his pad and pen back into his jacket pocket. "I guess I should go." He stayed where he was.

"No." Suddenly desperate, she put her hand out and touched his sleeve. *Don't leave yet. I don't care about Floyd Sanders. I want you here.* But she offered, "He may call again...."

He didn't move. Her hand stayed where she laid it. She repressed the urge to clutch his sleeve.

Finally Rand spoke in a heavy even tone. "I'll make sure Mr. Sanders realizes the consequences of any further harassment of any kind."

Again, they stood in tableau. Then Rand moved a step backward and Connie looked up into his eyes. The look she saw there was a revelation.

He's looking at me the way Jack looks at Gracie, the way Gil looks at Patience, the way Troy looks at Annie. It's the look of love. Rand loves me.

The thought stunned her.

"I guess I should be going," Rand said, but didn't move.

"No." She closed her hand over his wrist, the look in his eyes told her all she needed to know, all she needed to act. *I don't want you to go.* "Stay. Please." She swallowed, trying to moisten her dry mouth. "We'll talk."

"You want me to stay?" he said, sounding as if each word cost him.

"Yes." Then, daringly, she drew him along with her toward the love seat. The love seat where they had spent many evenings just sitting in each other's arms. She perched on the edge of the cushion, still clinging to his wrist.

For a moment, only a moment, he held back. Then he sank down beside her and pulled her near. "Connie," he murmured. "Connie."

A deep sigh flowed out of her and she snuggled closer against his firm chest, deeper into the cradle of his strong arms. "Rand."

Time passed. Connie felt and heard the beating of his heart under her ear. At first, it matched her own rapid pulse, and then it slowed to normal. Still, wonderfully, he didn't release her.

"I can't lose you," Rand finally murmured, amazed that he could say this aloud at long last.

"I'm not going anywhere." She looked up and smiled at him. "And I'm not letting you go, either."

"But…" He had to know. He had to ask her. He couldn't form a relationship with her if at the back of his mind… There was no subtle way to ask this. He braced himself. "Do you still have feelings for Troy?"

She stilled in his arms. She waited till her heart stopped throbbing again. She couldn't look at him.

"Tell me," he coaxed. "Get it out. Let it go."

She looked at him then. Moments passed.

What was she thinking? Had he pushed her too far? He had a hard time swallowing. "You don't owe me any explanation," he conceded.

That was certainly true.

But he noted a shift in her expression. Did she really want to tell him? He decided, he must wait in silence. If she wanted to tell him, then she would. If she could not, he wouldn't be able to commit completely to her because she wouldn't have committed to him.

She must tell him the truth, put whatever was in the past behind her, behind them. Seconds ticked by. He had a hard time breathing. Would they make it or not?

"I *was* in love with Troy." She stroked his cheek. "A long time ago. Before he married Annie."

Though expected, her confession stabbed into him, a dull blade of pain under his heart. "I know how it feels to let go of a past love," he whispered.

She pressed her cheek to his as though thanking

him. Then she feathered his hair away from his face, her touch comforting him. "I loved Troy even before he dated me in high school. When he broke up with me in our sophomore year, I acted like I didn't care. But it hurt." She paused and wouldn't meet his eyes.

He understood why. *You'd rather keep this secret, but you want someone to know, want me to know you've suffered, too.* He sat absolutely still, not wanting anything to stop the flow of her words, somehow waiting to share in the release she'd feel when she'd purged herself.

"Then Annie entered high school and he started dating her." Connie's voice wilted with regret. "I didn't let on that I still cared. I had no right to. Troy wanted Annie. Not me. And she was almost a sister to me."

Rand heard the anguish in her voice. He licked his dry lips. "What happened...what did you do when they got engaged?"

"I knew then that I had to stop loving him." Pulling away, she rubbed her arms as though they were freezing, though a warm breeze fluttered in through the sliding door. "If Annie married Troy, I knew it would be a sin to continue to have feelings for him."

That would matter to Connie. She wouldn't behave dishonorably to a friend...or enemy. "What did you do?" Rand finally asked.

"When I came home from college for Christmas, I faced the fact that I needed help to get rid of my feelings. I went and talked to our pastor. I told him the truth about…about how I felt about Troy. I asked him, 'I know he belongs to Annie now. How do I stop loving someone?'"

Rand echoed her question silently. Did he really still love Cara? Was it possible to love Connie as he had loved his wife? *Yes.*

"My pastor said," Connie continued, her head bent low, "that sometimes people become fixated on one person. Their feelings outlast the relationship. He said he'd seen this with people who had been divorced and still wanted to go back to their spouse no matter what."

"That makes sense." To have something to do with his hands, Rand stroked Connie's hair. "It must have been pretty tough on you to tell someone."

"It was, but it helped me put everything into perspective. He told me that it wasn't a sin to be attracted to Troy."

Rand caught her eye. "Even when Troy was going to marry someone else?"

She fingered her hair behind her ears, her fingers brushing his. Sparks flew up his arms from her touch. "The pastor said whom we are attracted to is something that is very hard to control since it comes from deep inside a person for reasons humans just don't understand. But he said I must take charge of my mind. My mind could lead me to sin."

Rand let his arm rest on the love seat, just inches from Connie. "What does that mean?"

"He read me the passage in Matthew, the Sermon on the Mount, where Christ taught about adultery, about having lustful thoughts." She stopped to sigh.

She leaned back against his shoulder and then rested one slender hand on the back of the love seat, just touching the sensitive skin on the back of his neck. "The pastor asked me if I would actually sin with Troy, knowing now he'd given his promise to Annie. I said no. I'd never hurt Annie, never commit a sin like that."

"So you didn't let yourself think about Troy?" Rand stared over at her, trying to make eye contact. He wanted to hear this. He wanted to tell her to stop.

"He said whenever I had thoughts about Troy, I had to consciously stop and turn my mind to other things. He told me never to imagine that Troy and I were anything but friends. He told me never to be alone with Troy."

"Did Troy or Annie ever guess you had feelings for him?" Rand stood up suddenly, gripped by a need to move.

"No, I don't think so. I've been very careful." She gazed at him, resting her head against the love seat. With her index finger, she traced the seam of the upholstery. "But I wasn't able to move on. I still felt the attachment, infatuation. For whatever reason. I can't explain it."

Rand shoved his hands into his pockets. "Maybe it had just become a habit." *Like my standing apart after losing Cara.*

"Maybe. But after Troy and Annie became engaged, I was never in love with Troy—not the way you said it that day in your driveway. I didn't…" She shook her head, looking down. "I'd accepted that he's happiest with Annie and the boys. But that night in the E.R. when I saw Troy, looking so…awful, my feelings for him changed. I finally saw him as…just Annie's husband. I don't know how to explain it, but it was as if someone had clipped a thread of my life and I was changed."

Rand nodded. He could understand that. It had been a shock, a life-changing moment.

"Before, when you and I argued, about whether Troy had been kidnapped or had run away," she said, "I just couldn't believe that Troy could betray Annie. I couldn't accept that he would treat her like that… leave her and his sons penniless. But that night, I saw that it was all true, terribly true. It was somehow like he'd betrayed me, too. That's stupid, I know."

"No, it isn't stupid." He moved to the love seat again.

"Do you remember how I reacted when we found out that Uncle Lou had paid protection money? When I said I should put away childish things like expecting perfection in the ones I love?"

"Yes." Rand wished he had comfort to give her.

"I was thinking that over last night and I recalled a verse I memorized a long time ago." She recited, " 'When I was a child, I talked like a child, I thought like a child, I reasoned like a child. When I became a man, I put childish ways behind me.' " She held up both arms to him, asking him to come close, to hold her. "Rand, I think I've finally put away my childish feelings for Troy. I'm free of my past infatuation over him now."

Rand took both her hands and drew her into his arms. He buried his face in her neck and rocked her gently.

"What about you?" Connie murmured into his ear.

He stilled. "What about me?"

"Are you still in love with your wife?" Her voice faltered.

"No." His voice didn't sound strong enough. He couldn't let her think that. He repeated it, "No."

She rubbed his arms with her hands. "Then what is it? What kept you fencing with me?"

He tucked her deeper into his embrace. "I think it wasn't that I still loved Cara. It was the pain…of losing her…in such a violent way. She didn't just die. She was kidnapped and murdered. I should have been able to protect her. I was a cop. And I couldn't even protect my own wife."

Connie lifted her face to his and kissed him—

once, twice. "We live in a world where terrible things happen to good people. I don't know why your wife had to die such a terrible death. But it wasn't your fault, none of it."

He held her tightly. Again, he heard the pastor's voice at little Michael's christening—*I assure you that whoever does not receive the Kingdom of God like a child will never enter it.... Christ told Nicodemus, "You must be born again."* Rand gazed down at the top of Connie's head and felt a rush of love that nearly weakened his knees. *I've been given a second chance, Lord, and I won't turn my back on her...or You. I'll believe that we have a chance to make it together in this harsh world.*

"What are you thinking?"

"I was just thanking God for you. I love you. I'm never letting you go."

She rose on tiptoe and kissed him again. "You'd better not. I want to hold you like this every evening for the rest of our lives."

He kissed her forehead, her eyes each in turn, and then lowered his mouth to hers. "I love you, Ms. Constance Oberlin, and I *will* hold you like this every night for the rest of our lives."

Epilogue

The following June, Connie balanced the two large brightly colored large but lightweight boxes in her arms as she negotiated the steps up to Annie's apartment. "It's me!" she called out and then paused as a wave of vertigo rushed through her, making her feel faint.

"Here, let me help you with those." Annie met her at the top of the steps, peering around the boxes. "Are you sure it's really Mrs. Rand O'Neill behind there?"

Connie chuckled, getting back her equilibrium. "Just Connie will do."

"How was the honeymoon?"

"I've been back well over a month." Connie let Annie take the top gift. "You could call me."

"We never get to talk anymore." Annie led her into the living room decorated with blue-and-pink crepe paper. "I had finals about the time you returned and I'm doing an internship. I'm sorry, Connie. I'm just so busy—"

"Yes, we're all so busy," a very pregnant Gracie agreed and hugged Connie. Then an equally pregnant Patience took her turn welcoming Connie.

Connie was busy with her new husband and new career in adoption law. Floyd Sanders had stopped harassing her, but she had decided she'd rather make her career in protecting children and creating families.

Soon the apartment was abuzz with chattering women. Finally, Annie stood up. "I'm so happy you all could come to Patience and Gracie's combined baby shower."

The women, many from the neighborhood, who had known Gracie since babyhood and Patience as a child, all clapped and called out happy comments.

"Before we start the games—" Annie halted as the back door slammed.

"Mommy!" her twins yelled. "Daddy says can he take us for ice cream?"

"Yes, anything!" Annie smiled even as she scolded. "Go. This is for ladies, not boys." Annie shooed the two back out of the living room. "Tell your father to keep you at the park for another hour."

Connie felt a cautious breath of relief. Uncle Lou had paid Troy's debts when Troy agreed to attend Gambler's Anonymous and go to counseling with

Annie. No charges had been pressed against Troy when parts from his truck had been found at a chop shop. Evidence there had proved that he hadn't stolen it.

Connie, along with Gracie and Patience, had talked Annie into giving Troy another chance. Troy was working unpaid overtime to repay his uncle and Annie was taking fewer subjects and working only part-time for Jack. Annie and Troy had managed to hold their family together though the road was still rough.

Finally, the baby shower games had been suffered through and the gifts had been opened. Annie and Connie served white buttercream cake and strawberry ice cream. The sickly sweet smell of the frosting made Connie's stomach lurch.

"No cake?" Mama Kalanovski, who owned the café down the street, gave Connie an assessing look. "And how long you been married?"

"Just six weeks," Connie said. "Why do you ask?"

"That's long enough." Mama nodded and several other of the ladies gave Connie interested glances.

Connie caught on. "No, no. Not possible."

Mama nodded knowingly. "You get you one of those tests like I see on TV at the drugstore. I bet you a free lunch at the Polska that you and that detective of yours are expecting."

Connie shook her head, resisting the idea.

The pounding of feet on the back steps interrupted the conversations.

"Mommy, look. Daddy got us popcorn instead." The twins charged into the room with two white paper sacks of the treat.

The aroma of buttered popcorn hit Connie's queasy stomach. She leaped up and ran for the bathroom, nearly colliding with Troy.

"Ha!" Mama Kalanovski announced with triumph. "I'm right. You'll see. My first time, my Joe had to butter his morning toast outside for months."

Patience and Gracie ran to the closed bathroom door. "Connie!" they shrieked. "This is wonderful. We're all going to be mothers together."

In reply, Connie only moaned. Since Rand was older than she and wanted to start their family right away, she and Rand had decided to let God decide when they would be parents. *Dear Lord, You couldn't have given me a couple of months?* Then she grinned, thinking of what Rand would say, what his family would say. And they'd have that free lunch on Mama Kalanovski, too—just as soon as she could keep lunch down, that is!

* * * * *

Dear Reader,

This is the last of my SISTERS OF THE HEART series. Each of the three friends, Gracie, Patience and Connie, has, at the end of this book, found her true love.

No one would have put Connie and Rand together except God. Connie was just starting her life and was very idealistic, while Rand was a seasoned detective and had become cynical about life. Both of them had lingering entanglements from the past, and both had to learn to let go of these in order to move ahead—freely.

None of us can live more than one day at a time. The past is beyond our control. We can never go back and redo things. And the future holds much that we couldn't even guess was coming. Sometimes we wish we could look forward. But fortunately, we aren't able to do that, really a blessing.

I hope you have enjoyed this series. I look forward to hearing from you if this story has touched your heart. Please visit my Web site www.booksbylyncote.com or send mail in care of Steeple Hill Books, 233 Broadway, Suite 1001, New York, NY 10279.

Blessings,

Lyn Cote

Take 2 inspirational love stories FREE!

PLUS get a FREE surprise gift!

Mail to Steeple Hill Reader Service™

In U.S.
3010 Walden Ave.
P.O. Box 1867
Buffalo, NY 14240-1867

In Canada
P.O. Box 609
Fort Erie, Ontario
L2A 5X3

YES! Please send me 2 free Love Inspired® novels and my free surprise gift. After receiving them, if I don't wish to receive anymore, I can return the shipping statement marked cancel. If I don't cancel, I will receive 4 brand-new novels every month, before they're available in stores! Bill me at the low price of $4.24 each in the U.S. and $4.74 each in Canada, plus 25¢ shipping and handling and applicable sales tax, if any*. That's the complete price and a savings of over 10% off the cover prices—quite a bargain! I understand that accepting the books and gift places me under no obligation ever to buy any books. I can always return a shipment and cancel at any time. Even if I never buy another book from Steeple Hill, the 2 free books and the surprise gift are mine to keep forever.

113 IDN DZ9M
313 IDN DZ9N

Name	(PLEASE PRINT)	
Address	. Apt. No.	
City	State/Prov.	Zip/Postal Code

Not valid to current Love Inspired® subscribers.

Want to try two free books from another series?
Call 1-800-873-8635 or visit www.morefreebooks.com.

* Terms and prices are subject to change without notice. Sales tax applicable in New York. Canadian residents will be charged applicable provincial taxes and GST. All orders subject to approval. Offer limited to one per household.

® are registered trademarks owned and used by the trademark owner and or its licensee.

INTLI04R   ©2004 Steeple Hill

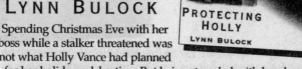